S

D1000435

94

Books by John Reese

BIG MUTT

SURE SHOT SHAPIRO

THE LOOTERS

SUNBLIND RANGE

PITY US ALL

SINGALEE

HORSES, HONOR AND WOMEN

JESUS ON HORSEBACK

BIG HITCH

SPRINGFIELD .45-70

SPRINGFIELD .45-70

By John Reese

14 S. D. B.

West

DOUBLEDAY & COMPANY, INC.

Garden City, New York

1972

All the characters in this book are fictitious, and any resemblance
to actual persons, living or dead, is purely coincidental.

ISBN: 0-385-08928-7
Library of Congress Catalog Card Number 72-79421
Copyright © 1972 by John Reese
All Rights Reserved
Printed in the United States of America
First Edition

For
Jack and Pat Victor,
affectionately.

SPRINGFIELD .45-70

CHAPTER ONE

They rode two and two, Mike Banterman and Clyde Fox well in the lead. The terrain had all been rolling grassland so far, dry and brown, and grazed too short to ripple in the chill fall wind. Now suddenly there were deep gullies, and brush and scrub trees. Prairie chickens burst from cover and took flight under the horses in nitwit panic. Two curious coyotes showed themselves boldly.

Where the wagon road curved, seeking a tamer grade, Mike reined in. His blue eyes twinkled at Clyde from a month's growth of black beard. "It galds me raw when a man asks me for a job like he's doing me a favor," he said. "Let's see how that aristocrat feels about things now."

He turned his thick body in the saddle to shout back over his shoulder, "Hey, Tidewater!"

The other two shook their horses into a trot. "Yes, sir, Mr. Banterman?" said one. His drawl somehow made it a polite but not necessarily sincere form of address. The words came out sounding like, "Yes, seh, Mist' Bant'man?"

"If you ever team to town," Mike said, "stick to the road. We'll take a short cut here, but it's a good place to get lost unless you know the trail."

"Once over a trail is gen'ly enough for me to learn it," the other replied.

He was a thin man, almost bony, with a fine big mustache half sandy and half gray. His high forehead was furrowed, giving him a peevish look, like an owl in sunlight. His heavy gray eyebrows met over eyes of an odd hazel shade, almost yellow. His thin beak of a nose had been burned red by the bottle or the sun—or both—but he was not a fall-down drunk.

He wore no coat, and his worn shirt was useless in the wind. His .45 was a good one and well cared for. His brown mare had the fine head and chest of hot blood, and he rode her with the Westerner's long stirrup but with a hard soldier rump in the saddle.

"Some men manage to get lost," Mike said. "I lease this land. Man that treats land like this, he don't deserve to own it. I'll own it someday, but it'll be forty years coming back."

"I see," the thin man replied.

"This is the kind of brush-poppin' work there is, until the snow blows. I told you it was nasty work, Tidewater, and there'll be no hard feelings if you change your mind."

The odd yellow eyes remained bland. "You don't

need to ride me to get the work done. I believe I mentioned that I don't like that name. I believe I told you, Mr. Banterman, that my name is Raitt."

"I didn't catch no first name, though."

Raitt hesitated long enough to make his point—that he did not confer the right to use his first name on everyone. "In the family, I'm called Eldon."

Mike grinned. "Fine with me, Mr. Raitt. I saw more of the Virginia aristocracy than I cared to, as a kid in the war. Maybe I'm tetchy about it. And my name is Mike. Nobody misters me on my place."

Raitt merely nodded. Mike looked at the other new man. "You're called Bru Hawley? What's the Bru for?"

"Brutus."

"Brutus, you're no working cowboy."

"I will be, tomorrow at this time."

"Where'd you learn to ride?"

"Mexico."

Mike studied him, seeing a man of twenty-two or -three, with a poise and gravity becoming a man of fifty. It was hard to say what kept him out of the average class, when he had such an average face and average build and clothing. But Mike had known other men who stood out in this same way. Usually he had learned to like and trust them.

"How'd you make your living in Mexico?"

"Stealing horses."

"Kind of a chancy trade, wasn't it?"

"There was a revolution on down there," Brutus Hawley replied. "I was called a *surtidor*. That means 'supplier.' You steal them from the other side."

"Which side was you on?"

"Well, both."

Mike whooped with laughter. Now he knew that he had no average man here. "Well, boys," he said, "we work hard on the Bar M, and winter's coming on. It's better for both of us if you decide right now that you don't want the job."

Behind him, Clyde Fox said, "Up at four-thirty for prayers, every day except Sunday. Then it's four. No cursing, chewing, or thinking dirty thoughts, and I still don't know what color Mike's barn is, because I've never seen it by daylight."

Bru Hawley grinned. Raitt made a polite smile. Clyde, expecting more, became silent. He was in his early twenties too—nondescript and forgettable. Whatever made Bru Hawley stand out, Clyde Fox lacked it.

"Let's git for home then," Mike said.

Raitt and Hawley again fell in behind the other two. "He likes his little joke, Mr. Banterman does," Raitt said peevishly.

"It's only a month or so," said Hawley. "Two, if we're lucky and the snow holds off. Then we're on

our way to Hermosillo—and no stops in El Paso this
time!"

Raitt gritted his teeth. "El Paso. I'll meet that son-
of-a-bitching bartender sometime," he said. "Nobody loads my whiskey and steals my poke and gets
away with it."

"Only it's so much trouble, when you finally get
around to it."

"Not for me. Not for me!"

A few miles on, it had grown so dark that Mike
and Clyde had to wait for them. In another hour, the
lights of the Bar M came into view. Bru Hawley sized
it up respectfully. Mr. Banterman had himself more of
a town than a cow ranch here.

Dogs ran out to bark a welcome. The rail at the
big, low house would tie thirty horses, at least. Beyond,
among live-oak and cottonwood trees, were barns,
sheds, and endless corrals. He could hear windmills
creaking, and an army of Mexican children ran out to
escort them to the bunkhouse. Mike talked to them
in bad but fluent Spanish and gave one of the older
ones a bag of candy from his saddle pouch to divide
among them.

"Where do we put up our horses?" Raitt said.
"Kind of like to have mine fed a little grain."

"Ride right up to the bunkhouse. Somebody will

take care of your horse for you, and grain her. That's how we do things here," Mike replied.

Every window glowed in the big stone bunkhouse. A one-legged stable hand came out to take their horses. A cook's helper in a clean white undershirt and clean apron appeared in the door, to hold it open for them.

"Set four places," Mike told him, leading the way through the bunkhouse. "Find empty bunks anywhere, boys, and then let's eat. The grub here ain't much, but it's nice and dirty."

"I notice you hog your share," the kitchen hand said.

Mike grinned and called out, "Couple of new farm boys that think they'd like to be cowboys! Give them a good old Bar M welcome, boys."

A groan arose from the thirty or more men in the bunkhouse. There was a big stove at each end, and tables where riders were playing cards. Bru Hawley noticed that at least half the men were Mexicans, as he and Raitt followed Mike on into the dining room. Mike sat down near the end of one of the big tables. Clyde sat down beside him.

Bru Hawley and Raitt sat on the benches opposite them. The cook's helper set out big bowls of warmed-over beef cooked with chili, brown beans fried with onions and cheese, baked squash, and cornbread with real butter. The two new men exchanged surprised looks. The Bar M fed well!

"Go tell Woody I want him," Mike said to the kitchen helper.

The man went out. He was back in a minute or two, followed by a huge Negro—a man at least six feet six in height, with a frame that carried two hundred and fifty pounds of solid brawn. His bare head was gray, but he walked with the quick slouch of a strong young man.

"You's back late," he said in a deep-bass voice.

"Yes. Hired you a couple of men, Woody," said Mike. "Put them in the brush tomorrow. We're racing the snow, and every day counts. Every cow counts. Run their tails off!"

"Sho'ly." The black man frowned. "You get me out of a warm house just to tell me this?"

"That's what I did."

"Oh, hell." The Negro grinned at Raitt and Hawley. "I find you horses in the morning. Don't guess I'll have to saddle 'em for you."

"Woody," Mike said, "notice Mr. Raitt's horse. Prettiest little Kentucky mare you ever seen."

"Sho'ly." The black man looked again at the two new men. "See you in the morning. *Buenas noches*."

It was Hawley who replied, "*Buenas noches*."

Woody went out. Mike said, "His name is Woody Brown. Best gang boss in Texas. Woody gets the work done, and he don't break your back doing it."

"That nigra is your foreman?" said Raitt.

"Yes. He's married to a nice little Mexican girl. They got a house of their own here. Woody is—"

"You expect me to work for a *nigra?*" Raitt said in a shrill, quivering voice.

He dropped his fork on his plate with a clang. He stood up and leaned across the table. Mike Banterman did not look up.

"If you work here, you do," he said.

"Maybe you meant this for a joke."

"Meant what for a joke?"

"You funned me all day about the Tidewater. You couldn't help but know how we feel about things, seh."

"Mr. Raitt, I don't care a damn how you feel about things. The war has been over nearly twenty-two years. You lost, in case you forgot."

"Mighty small potatoes, Mr. Banterman."

"What is?"

"Insulting a man that only asked you for a job, just because you won the war, seh?" Raitt said, his voice rising queerly at the end.

Mike stood up too. "I didn't win," he said harshly. "I fought three and a half years in the Army of Northern Virginia, because I was a kid with no better sense. I never owned no blacks. Hell, until that war was over I never even owned a horse! But I let your goddam

Tidewater planters whoop me into it, like they whooped their dogs onto a stray shote."

"It pleasures you to insult me, don't it?" Raitt almost whimpered. "I'm not the first man you've done this to, Mr. Banterman."

"No, you're not. I took too much from the planters' goddam boy officers, to forgive and forget. Let me tell you about that war, Mr. Raitt. We won all the battles, but we lost the war. Do you know why? It was us white-trash riflemen that won the battles, but your high-assed Tidewater officers lost the war after they got enough of us killed off."

"And you're glad they did!"

Mike said wearily, "I'm glad they did. Finish your supper, Mr. Raitt, and rest your horse so you can leave tomorrow. And if you don't like my idee of a good joke, remember one thing: Next time you ask a Texas man for a job, don't look down your nose at him like he had lice."

"You're a small man in your heart, seh."

"I reckon. You was an officer?"

"Captain."

"I was a sergeant at eighteen. I reckon you're right, Mr. Raitt—I treated you small, and I apologize. But the way you looked down at me when you hit me up for work—by God, will you people never learn?"

It was silent for a moment. Mike looked at Hawley, who had stopped eating.

"How about you, Mr. Hawley—you too proud to take orders from a black man?"

"If I have to decide now," Hawley said, "I'll quit. I don't like to be hustled."

"Nobody's hustling you. I need men, but you work for a black man. Everybody that works here, they say he's easy to work for. That's how we do things here."

He nodded good night and stalked out of the room. Clyde Fox looked up as he went on eating.

"Your boss has got some strong notions," Hawley said softly.

"Well, yes," said Clyde.

"He surely packs a grudge a long time."

"Well, he got all shot to hell in that war. And I'll tell you this—Woody Brown, he's easy to work for. Best boss I ever had."

"I cain't eat no more," Raitt said, and held out his hand. Bru Hawley put tobacco and papers into it. Raitt made a cigarette, lighted it, and walked out of the room.

All but one of the bunkhouse lamps had been blown out, and it had been turned down. Bru slipped into his Mackinaw and went down the back path to the toilet, one last time. The wind was not strong, but it had the cutting edge of a knife. He was almost trotting as he returned to the bunkhouse through the dark.

"Bru!" came a soft voice.

It was Raitt, standing humped under a tree with his hands in his pockets. Bru stopped beside him.

"Right wintry, this wind," he said.

"You going to work for a nigra?"

"It don't bother me, what color he is."

"I thought we's going to Hermosillo."

"How can we? We're broke."

"I counted on you, Bru. You's kind of letting me down if you work here, ain't you?"

"If you're sharing out the blame, Eldon, it wasn't me that wanted one more roaring drunk in El Paso. And if color's a matter of principle with you, stay out of Mexico! They're dark people too, and you do have a way of making somebody's hair stand on end."

Raitt's teeth chattered so hard he had to wait until he had controlled them. "Listen, though."

"What?"

"Banterman was in the bunkhouse. He hasn't paid this crew since June, you know that? I heard him tell them they could draw ten dollars apiece on Friday, and take Saturday off and go into town to buy their winter clothes."

"What about it?"

"Why, look at the size of this crew! He'll have more than three hundred dollars on him. That'd get us to Hermosillo in style. Listen, we ride out of here in the morning. Friday, we lay for this son of a bitch in the brush somewhere, and take that money and put him afoot. We're across the border and long gone before anybody misses him."

"I reckon not, Eldon."

"I thought you had nerve!"

Bru scuffed the path with the toe of his boot. "Not that kind, I reckon."

"You'd rather work for a nigra?"

"I told you, I don't care what color he is. My grandma, they said she was half black. Her mammy was a slave."

Raitt's strong teeth began chattering again. "You're a goddam nigra yourself! You didn't tell me that, Bru."

"You didn't tell me you's white trash, either."

"White trash? Why, you—"

Bru did not bother to raise his hands as Raitt fumbled for his gun. He shouldered Raitt back against the tree and said softly, "White trash! Maybe you could fool Mr. Banterman, but not no old Arkansas boy like me. I see right through you! Now you go inside, Eldon, before you freeze to death here."

Raitt made a whimpering sound of fury in his throat and went scuffing down the path to the bunkhouse.

The door closed behind him. In a moment, Bru followed slowly.

He opened the bunkhouse door carefully and took a careful look before stepping inside. Raitt had already found the bootjack across the room and was fitting his heel into it to remove his first boot. He did not look at Hawley, but when Bru got into his own bunk he slipped his .45 under his pillow and then lay down with his back to the wall.

When he woke up in the morning, when the bell rang at daylight, Raitt was already gone.

CHAPTER TWO

Mike Banterman's weight of guilt grew with every step as he made his way to the house. Oh, lordie, he thought, I done it again, and Velma is just going to give me hell for it . . . !

They had been making pickles that day, and his house was full of the winy odor of vinegar boiled with spices and sugar. Socorra, one of the elderly kitchen maids, was on her knees, polishing the tile floor of the kitchen. She moved aside for him.

"*Buenas noches, Señor*," she said.

"*Muy buenas noches*," he replied gruffly.

Socorra had been with him fifteen years. Two of her sons rode for him. She would have died for him, but, for his wife, who had not bothered to learn Spanish, she would cheerfully work her fingers to the bone. She was Velma's maid now, not his.

He did not have to ask where *la Señora* was. He could hear Velma at the piano that had been handed down through her goddam family since Noah was a second-class petty officer. He tried to go down the narrow back hall without being seen, but she had stationed herself at the piano for one reason only. To waylay him.

"Oh, Michael, there you are!" she called.

"Be right back. I want to wash off the trail dust," he called, and hurried on.

One final chord of exasperation, and she was after him. It was an oblong ebony grand piano that had cost Mike six hundred dollars to ship from Louisiana. It took ten men to lift it, and then he had to go under the house and shore up the floor with stone pillars to hold it.

She had made him build a dressing room and bath off their bedroom. He was filling a basin when she came up behind him and said, "I kept water hot for your bath, Michael dear."

"I'm too tired for a bath," he said, without looking around. "I'll just get rid of the dust."

"Oh, no, you can't come to bed like that! You must shave, too. Oh, yes, I know—nobody shaves during roundup. Only you'll be two more months if the snow holds off, and you look like a bull buffalo."

"God Almighty," he moaned.

Defeated, he turned to face her. Mike was forty-five, and for thirty of those years—two thirds of his life-time—he had been a camp stag. First in the Confederate States Army and then building up his herds and his money until he could buy the Bar M. A hard life, but a good one. A man's life.

He had thrown it all away to answer an ad in a matrimonial magazine picked up in an Austin barbershop:

> GENTLEWOMAN, thirty, no fortune, plantation background, good family & education in arts, music, literature. Said to be attractive. Will consider marriage to gentleman of similar tastes & accomplishments with income for secure but not luxurious life.

In a convulsion of madness he had written a letter that began, "I am not a gentleman. I can read and write only because I learned how, to run my own business. Also my family are said by some to be white trash, but not in my hearing. However I have to ride 30 miles to cross my own land, & maybe 6000 head cattle wear my brand."

The hell of it was, her ad was as truthful as his response—and what a beauty she was! Could not cook, sew, keep a garden or chickens, or even comb her own hair. Get all there was to be got out of servants. Pretty up a house, a table, or a bed.

Hair like new-threshed wheat straw, skin so white it looked like marble, yet eyes so dark they were smoky. Eyes that saw right through him, every time.

"You're not going to bed until you shave and bathe, Michael. I'll fill the tub for you."

"I'll sleep in the bunkhouse."

"You'll sleep in your own bed, but no one is too tired to want to be clean. Get undressed now."

She took clean underwear out of a drawer for him and laid it on a chair. She picked up the pail that stood beside the stove.

"All right, but I can fill my own goddam tub," he said.

She ignored anything he said that included profanity. He watched helplessly while she filled the tub from the boiler on the stove.

"Let me have your soiled things now, Michael."

Soiled, not dirty. "Dirty" was white-trash talk. He peeled off his clothes and let her have them, and started toward the tub.

"Oh, no!" she cried. "Shave first."

"I told you, I'm—oh, all right!"

She went out and closed the door. He lathered his beard and rinsed it again and again. He lathered it one last time and let it soak while he stropped the razor.

He heard the piano again as he got into the tub. She was still playing when he came down the hall, buckling the belt of his clean pants. She smiled at him, but she finished the piece she was playing. He leaned across the piano to watch her.

"I did it again," he said, when the music had come to an end.

"Did what?" his wife replied. "I knew you were up to something, but what?"

"I hired some busted-down Tidewater planter today, and I rode his tail hard." He told her about Raitt. "Honest to God, Velma—I swear every time I'm not going to do it. And then one of them sons of bitches —excuse that, hon—one of them *aristocrats* looks down his nose at me—"

"They're not aristocrats if they look down their noses at you."

He waved his big hand at her. "Maybe not to you. But I was an enlisted man. This fella hit me up for a job like it was really below him, but he was in a mood to be nice to the poor folks. He did everything but holler at me, 'Hey, boy!' And I tell you, hon, I was just as bad as he was. I did everything but take him into Eli Porter's bank and show him my money."

"Don't let people like that upset you, Michael. You're a bigger man than that."

He squinted blindly into a shadowy corner of the room. "I reckon an old soldier never really puts his war behind him. There's a certain kind of man—well, I just go wild, and I can't help it."

She got up and came around the piano, smiling a

little. "You know what you have to do, Michael. Apologize to him!"

"Apologize to who?"

"Your Tidewater man."

"I'll see him in hell first! Besides, I already did."

"I know about how you did it. This time, really mean it. Get it out of your heart, because you won't sleep all night unless you do. You were just as overbearing to him as your officers used to be to you, and the poor man has to take it from you, just as you did. You're ashamed, and you should be!"

He winced, but he took both her hands in his and smiled sheepishly. "I reckon you're right. I'll catch him first thing in the morning."

"No, now. You won't sleep if you don't."

He went out, but he was soon back. His wife was standing at the fireplace. She saw the look on his face and smiled again.

"You didn't do it!"

"No. The minute I seen his face, I couldn't say a word. It ain't my imagination this time, Velma. He purely despises me for white trash! I thought of Woody Brown, and I couldn't do it. Woody worked for me when nobody else would trust me to find their wages, and by God, I wasn't going to beg no man's pardon that looks down on Woody and me both."

"What did you do, just walk out?"

"No. Like a fool, I made out that I came out to tell everybody they could take next Saturday off and go into town to buy winter clothes. I had to say something. Now I've got to go in Friday and get them some money. Ain't that the limit?"

"Then forget your Tidewater man," Velma said, leaning against him. "Just stay away from people like that, Michael dear. You'll never change them, and all they can do is cause you trouble."

"Trouble?" Mike said, taking her into his arms. "What trouble could the likes of him cause to me?"

CHAPTER THREE

Raitt burrowed into the warm blankets and was instantly asleep. He was in bad shape. He had been on short rations for weeks. He had got drunk and taken an overdose of knockout drops in El Paso, and had been closer to dying than Bru had known. The helpless rage caused by Banterman's trick, and then the humiliating discussion with Bru, had used up the last of his strength.

He slept deeply, like a sick man, but he awakened instantly when the cook's helper shook down the fires at three in the morning. For a moment he did not realize where he was. I've got to get out of here, he thought when he recognized Banterman's bunkhouse. I said too much to Bru. The nigras stick together. . . .

He dressed beside the stove, longingly looking at the warm Mackinaw hanging on Bru's bunk. He knew better than to steal it. That would bring the whole Bar M outfit after him like a pack of hounds.

Shivering in his thin shirt, he groped his way to the kitchen. "Where'll I find my horse?" he said.

"You leaving?" said the cook. "Better eat first. Mr. Banterman don't want nobody to leave here hungry."

"The hell with him!" said Raitt.

"Don't take his joshing too hard. He's just a big overgrown boy, and that's the truth! Set down at my own little table there. Coffee's nigh done, and I'll find you something to eat. You'll feel better, my friend, with a full gut."

Raitt could not resist it. The hot food and coffee restored his strength, but he did not feel better. The cook talked endlessly about Mr. Banterman. You got along with him same as you did a loud-mouthed kid. No kinder man in the world, under that loud talk!

The cook gave Raitt an old denim jacket and showed him where to find his horse. The crew was just rising when Raitt cantered out, taking the road south because the chill wind was in the north.

The sun was high, but the wind just as cold when he rode through the gullied place where Banterman had pointed out the danger of getting lost. If a man was going to stick Banterman up, this was the place to do it. But something told him that sticking Banterman up would be more than a one-man job.

He thought bitterly of Bru. His hatred of Bru was deeper than his hatred of Banterman, for two reasons. One was the African blood that Bru had concealed while they were trail pards. Raitt would never live that down. The other was that white-trash taunt. Only a nigra could make it sting like that.

Long before he was close to town, Raitt left the trail and rode eastward before turning south again. He did not know where he was going, but he did not want to be seen again in the town where Banterman had hired him.

Raitt had never been a fugitive from the law, but he had a fugitive's well-honed instincts. When the world got to be too much for him, he withdrew from it. He did not want to be seen by men, then. No telling how long these spells lasted. Finally he got drunk and stayed drunk, this being the only way a man could really leave the world behind. Coming out of a long drunk, he could rejoin mankind again for a while.

Down there somewhere was the Rio Grande, and beyond it, Mexico. Somewhere down there was Hermosillo, where Bru Hawley said it was always warm. That was one more dream he could put behind him. He would never dare to venture into Mexico alone.

Early in the afternoon, he caught a flash of movement ahead of him. He had seen nothing but cattle all day, but this was no cow critter. He pulled the mare down and stood up in the stirrups to squint suspiciously across the brush-covered hills.

There it was again—a spotted horse, the kind these ignorant Texans called a paint or a pinto, and it was hobbled. It disappeared into a gully. Raitt nudged the mare into a walk.

Soon he saw the pinto again. A hobbled horse meant somebody camped nearby. Raitt dismounted and led the mare cautiously. The pinto was plump—downright fat, to tell the truth. An expensive gelding, but all looks. Not half the horse his little mare was.

He tied the mare in the bottom of a gully and walked ahead with his hand on his gun. In a minute, he saw them, two men beside a small campfire. One was asleep. The other sat facing the fire with his knees drawn up, his arms around his legs, his chin resting dejectedly on one knee.

Raitt sized them up a long time before he began walking boldly down toward them. There was no question in his mind about one thing. They were hiding out from something, but they were not very wary about it. Without half trying, Raitt could have come up on them and got the drop from behind.

Instead, when he was still several hundred yards away, he stopped and put both hands on his hips, in plain sight. "Afternoon there, y'all by the fire," he called.

The sleeping one went on sleeping. The other one twisted like a snake as he hit the ground. He came up with a rifle clutched to his side. It was the biggest rifle Raitt had ever seen.

"Who are you? What do you want?" he yelled back in a taut, frightened voice.

Just a kid, Raitt decided—some runaway due for a whipping if he got caught with his pappy's gun and horse. Somehow, all of Raitt's self-confidence came back in a surge. His luck had changed.

"Sho', now, put up that cannon!" he called back, elevating his hands. "Look, you got the drop on me. All I want is to warm up and eat a bite with you, if you can spare something."

"We ain't got nothing to eat ourselves."

"You got a rifle, though," Raitt said, walking slowly toward the kid. "Brush is full of calves. My, but that's a beautiful gun! What is it, that new Army Springfield?"

The chinless, pimple-faced youth stood there and let him walk right up to the fire. "Yes, and it's my gun," he said. "I got a bill of sale to prove it."

Raitt showed his fine white teeth under his big mustache in a man-to-man smile. "How about the pinto? You got a bill of sale for him too?"

"I sure have! I worked all summer in the damn Louisiana swamps for that horse and this gun."

"You don't have to lie to me, boy. Why, I surely don't care where you got your rifle and your horse!"

"I ain't lying, God dang it! I kin show you the bills of sale."

The sleeping man went on sleeping. He was not much older than the youth with the rifle, but he was dead drunk. He had vomited all over himself, and would wake up wishing himself dead.

"Why, *I* don't care about your bills of sale, or where you got the money to buy your gun and your horse, boy!" Raitt said.

"I told you, I worked all—"

"I know what you told me, but you never made wages enough cutting cypress to buy a fine gun like this, and a fine pinto horse. When did you eat last?"

The kid was half starved, with a drunken partner on his hands and a story that did not quite hang together. Raitt kept smiling at him, a little contemptuously but without antagonism. It was easy to make friends, to take command. Shortly the kid was handing over the big rifle for the admiring Raitt to examine.

It was a Springfield .45-70, a bolt-action rifle that would throw a slug as big as a man's thumb a quarter of a mile—with accuracy, if the man firing it had a steady eye and a firm grip. Raitt knew guns. He had heard about the Springfield, and knew that the Army was issuing them to some crack infantry regiments. But he had never handled one before.

They walked back to where he had tied the little mare, the kid carrying the gun. The kid's pale eyes widened at sight of the mare.

"How old is she?"

"Going on six, I reckon."

"How much hot blood?"

"All, my friend! She's from flat-racing stock, bred in southeastern Kentucky. I wouldn't ride a tramp horse. Now let me have the rifle, and I'll go get us a fat calf."

"Oh, no! Nobody shoots my rifle but me."

"Afraid I'll steal it? Here, you hold my horse, lad. She's worth a dozen of your guns."

"The hell she is! This gun cost me—"

"I know about how much your gun cost you. Did you ever ride a fifteen-hundred-dollar horse? You got any idee how fast this horse runs a mile? Sho', boy, you're just talking ridiculous!"

The kid would believe anything. He followed slowly on Raitt's mare, keeping well back, while Raitt stalked calves. Raitt let several of them get away, because they were easy shots. The heavy rifle thrilled and fascinated him. He wanted to test it at close to its limit, and test himself at the same time.

He brought down a fat weaned calf with one shot through the ribs, from so far away that it fetched a piercing whistle of admiration from the kid. When Raitt got out his pocket stockmen's knife to stick the calf, the kid tumbled out of the saddle.

"No, use this," he said, drawing a knife from a sheath

that he wore under his shirt. "This is a real fighting knife, what they call a four-three. It's made in Cuba, and—"

"I cut my teeth on fighting knives."

They bled the calf. They took both hindquarters back with them, tied across the mare behind the saddle. They walked slowly, Raitt carrying the rifle. I need this gun, Raitt kept telling himself. But let's take it slow now, because maybe I need this trashy kid too. . . .

Skillfully he led the kid to tell him most of what he wanted to know about himself. The rest, Raitt could guess.

His name was Eph Crippen, he was nineteen years old, and this was his home town. His pappy was Shep Crippen, who had no trade except drinking. His mother had been dead for years. Eph had run off last winter, nearly a year ago, to make his own way in the world. He had saved his money for the thing that meant the most to him, a good horse.

The young drunk asleep by the fire was Bobby Fayette, who also had been a teamster in the cypress groves. Raitt surmised that it was Fayette who had planned whatever paltry stick-up that had got Eph the money to buy the gun. Now, both were broke. Eph at least had a gun and a horse. Bobby Fayette had already drunk up his share.

Nearing the camp again, Raitt stopped and put his hand on Eph's shoulder for a man-to-man talk. "You get rid of this here Fayette, Eph," he said. "I'll show you how to cash in some real money if you got a little nerve. You don't get rich dragging saw logs out of no cypress swamp. I'll show you how to take it away from somebody, just as easy as pie."

"Stick up somebody?"

"That's what they call it. Man that can't hang onto his money don't deserve it, hey? You and me, we'll make a hell of a team. Run that Fayette off before he gets you into trouble somewhere."

"No. I couldn't do that. Bobby's my pal."

Raitt let it drop there. Eph had not balked at the words "stick up." They walked the rest of the way to the meager camp. Fayette was still asleep, but he stirred and moaned softly now and then.

Raitt borrowed Eph's fighting knife again, to slice thin slivers of meat that would broil quickly over a small fire. They squatted on their heels and gorged themselves on an amazing amount of delicious meat. The rifle lay between them, but Raitt had put it down in a position where it was a handy grab for himself. If Eph went for it, he would have to snatch it up in his left hand, turn it over, and swing it across his body before he could aim and fire it.

They did not talk about the stick-up. Eph tried

twice to tiptoe up to the subject. Each time, Raitt smilingly shook his head and threw a rueful glance at Fayette. Not with him here, that look said.

Late in the afternoon, Fayette made several attempts to get to his feet. On one of them, he made it. He was bigger than he had looked, with the adenoidy, truculent look of a street bully. The sides of his pants, under his belt, had been chafed by a gun belt, but he wore none now. It had gone to buy booze, probably.

"Who are you?" he said to Raitt in a hoarse, hangover voice. He tried hard to bring his eyes into focus, in a head that was pounding with pain.

Raitt looked at Eph. "Where did this scum leave his horse?"

Eph looked down at the ground. "Bobby hasn't got no horse. We rode double this fur."

"No horse! Eph, what kind of pardner hasn't even got a horse? Get rid of him."

"No." Eph licked his lips. "Why don't you just ride on and let us be?"

Raitt chuckled silently, making Eph cringe. Fayette tried hard to make contact with whatever was going on around him.

"I asked you a question," he said. "You son of a bitch, who are you?"

Raitt's eyes narrowed. He drew his gun, slowly and deliberately, making sure that Fayette saw him do it.

He then took quick and careless aim at Fayette's boot heel, from perhaps fifteen feet away.

He was not that good a shot, but today he was a lucky one. The drunk howled with terror as the shock of the bullet traveled through the boot. He thought he was wounded, and when he stepped down on the heelless boot and lost his balance, he knew he was.

Raitt sat there with the gun in his hand and let Fayette get to his hands and knees. He waved the gun at him.

"Start walking," he said softly.

Fayette looked at Eph. Eph looked down at the ground and took another bite of meat. Raitt tensed his whole body suddenly and squeezed off another shot. Fayette heard it go past his ear. He got up and started walking. He limped badly, with only one heel.

He stopped twice to try to throw up, while he was still close enough for them to hear the sound of his agony. The third time, Raitt picked up the Springfield and took careful aim. He did not hit the other boot heel this time, but he came close enough to convince Fayette.

"Very nice gun," Raitt said, putting the rifle down again.

Eph said nothing. They sat there and watched the man stumble out of sight.

"Well rid of him, Eph."

"What'll he do? He's a fur piece from anywhere."

"Die, probably. What in heaven's name were you going to do with the likes of him, anyway?"

"Well, we was going to pick us up a little money, and a good horse for Bobby and head down into Mexico."

"What would you do down there?"

"I worked down there quite a bit. I know some folks there."

My luck has changed, yes, indeed it has. . . . "Ever been to Hermosillo?"

"Oh, no. That's in Sonora, ain't it? I only been in Chihuahua."

"You speak the language?"

"Well enough. If they talk too fast, I got to slow them down. But I kin get by."

"That's where we're going, after we pull this little stick-up I told you about. Hermosillo!"

"Who you planning to stick up?"

"Do you know a man by the name of Banterman?"

"Mike Banterman? Jesus, who don't? He's about the richest man around here!"

"We ain't going to dip into his wealth very deep. Just enough to get us to Hermosillo and keep us in comfort and style for a while. There's money to be made there, boy!"

Eph thought it over and shook his head. "I don't

think I could stick up Mike Banterman. The son of a bitch, I tried to work for him twice. I—him and me, we just didn't hit it off."

"You mean you're skeered of him."

"No, I ain't skeered of him!"

"Yes, you are, but don't you worry about that," Raitt said soothingly. "I got this planned so it's easy for you and easy for me. We got until Friday. That's when he'll have the money. Is anybody likely to turn up out here and see us? Maybe we ought to saddle up and make camp somewhere else until Friday."

"Well," Eph said uncertainly, "I sure don't owe Mike Banterman anything, but it makes me nervous just to think of facing him down with a gun. I don't think I could do it."

"You don't have to do it. I'm going to do it with this rifle. What's the use of a fine gun like this if you don't get some use from it?"

"No. Nobody uses my rifle!"

Raitt picked up the rifle and stood up. "Let's mosey along and make a better camp. Go catch your horse and saddle up. We'll pick up the rest of our calf before the coyotes get to it. Man don't need anything else for a few days, with plenty of meat."

Eph said nothing more about the rifle. He was born to obey, Raitt thought, just as I was born with the gift of command. . . . He waited beside his mare, the rifle in his hand, while Eph shambled away to catch the hobbled pinto. He hefted the gun appreciatively. Heavy, yes, but unbeatable for the job it was designed for—to kill men at the maximum distance. It threw a slug forty-five hundredths of an inch in diameter, with the force of seventy grains of powder behind it. Sight adjustable two ways, for windage and trajectory.

"I don't even know your name," Eph said, not meeting Raitt's eyes, as they mounted.

"The name is Raitt. With two t's. R, a, i, t, t. And that's my real name, Eph. Where I come from, it's a name of consequence and standing."

"What's your first name, though?"

"Eldon; but you better just call me 'Mister Raitt,' Eph. Let's get started out right."

CHAPTER FOUR

"I like to see that," said State Senator Aubrey Chidester. "A man that's in love with his wife, I mean."

Sheriff Casey Oaks watched the rig go out of sight up the street, Mike Banterman slouched in the seat, his big black foreman driving the team. The horses knew they were going home. They would run as long as Woody would let them run.

"He's sure-enough in love with her, all right," the sheriff said. "They make a good pair."

"Certainly do. I'm glad I finally got to meet him. I knew his wife before they were married, you know. Fine old Louisiana family. She has fit herself into Texas pretty well, I should judge."

"Yes, she has. Come inside where it's warm, Aub."

The sheriff opened the door to his office, which was in the bottom of the courthouse at the rear. He made a little courtesy bow, which Senator Chidester returned before going in first.

A nod from the sheriff, and a young deputy working at a desk in the far corner of the room got up and reached for his hat. It was Friday, almost noon, and time for young men to be eating. The two older ones had breakfasted late. They sat down, the sheriff behind his desk, the senator in the deputy's swivel chair, which he dragged across the room.

"Well, what do you think of him, Aub?" the sheriff said.

"Of Banterman? Handsome man; personable in a crude, roughneck way; tremendous energy and a nimble mind. What does he want, anyway? You didn't keep him here, talking his head off for me, for nothing," Senator Chidester said.

"You better ask him what he wants."

"Then let's put it another way, Casey. What do *you* want?"

Sheriff Casey Oaks leaned on his desk, his big head with its big hooked nose and drooping mustache as motionless as granite. He stared blindly at nothing, ignoring a big green fly that had survived the first fall weather, and that swooped and circled around that bald spot on the back of his head. The senator waited.

Casey was forty-nine years old. He carried no fat, and there was no gray in his mustache. It was the slump of his shoulders, the sloth of his movements, that made him a changed man. To the senator, here was a man who had quit squandering himself purposelessly. Every thought, movement now had a good reason.

"What do I want?" said Casey. "I want to go back

to Austin, and this time I ain't going to take 'no' for an answer."

"Anything particular in mind?"

"Ferris Terry's job, in the auditor's office."

"Hm! First things first. What are you going to do with Ferris?"

"He's been in there eighteen years. He's been taking money for seventeen and a half of them. Nothing big, but it's been steady. He bought the Rice place near San Angelo, and I reckon that's no news to you.

"No; hear me out! He paid twelve thousand cash for that place. He didn't steal it from funds that went through his office. He has made some good investments, but not that good. He had to have money to invest in the first place, Aub.

"Point is, Ferris has had his share plus a little more. I'm at an age where I don't want to get rich, now that Blanche is dead. I want to take it easy, and I want to be back in Austin."

"Vindication," the senator murmured.

"Whatever you call it, I mean to have it."

"That sounds like an ultimatum."

"It is one," the sheriff said quietly.

"Why didn't you seek it while your wife was still alive? It was her name too. She—"

"She stood the disgrace all them years, and stuck with me," the sheriff said harshly. "This damn dreary cow town killed her. Nobody she could talk to, until Mike Banterman married an educated woman. I could stand anything too, as long as she lived. I tried to live it down, for her sake. Now, I see it wasn't a kindness to her. I should've done it while she was still alive, only—"

"Only she wouldn't let you," the senator cut in sharply.

The fly touched down on Casey's bald spot. His hand came up, fast as a striking snake. He had to take out his handkerchief to wipe the crushed fly off his head, and the senator noticed with a twinge of pity that it was not a clean handkerchief. While Blanche was alive, Casey never left the house without a clean one.

"No, she wouldn't let me. I don't give a damn what anybody says about me. But now, when they walk past Blanche's grave, by God I mean for them to know she wasn't the wife of a thief! You tell the Governor that."

The senator studied him thoughtfully. He had never known Sheriff Oaks to bluff. "I wonder," he said, "how Mike Banterman fits into this?"

"Either I get that job or I run Mike for Congress."

The senator flinched. "Jesus! You come out with both hammers cocked, don't you? Can you elect him?"

"I wouldn't run him if I couldn't."

"Yes, that boyish enthusiasm, that bull drive would

look good on a platform. He'd be a tireless cam-
paigner."

"The perfect candidate."

Senator Chidester sighed. "Well, I can tell His Nibs.
I can terrify him with the thought of a congressman he
can't handle. But I can't make him give you that
job."

"Don't nobody ever forget?" Oaks burst out.

"Not something that disgraces the Texas Rangers.
Casey, have you ever talked to Colonel Crawford?
Have you any idee how he feels about you?"

"After all these years? Blamed for something I never
done—a disgrace I don't deserve?"

"*¡Al otro perro, este hueso!*"

The sheriff half stood up, fists clenched, teeth bared
under his mustache in a snarl of fury. The sneering
old Spanish saying—"Throw that bone to some other
dog"—hit him as nothing else could have.

"I can't lie to the Governor, damn it, Casey!" the
senator said, shaking his finger in Casey's face. "He
knows—and Colonel Crawford knows—and *you* know
—the truth. The reason Blanche never let you make
a fight for vindication was that you were guilty as
hell! You took that money."

Eleven years before, Lieutenant Casey Oaks of the
Texas Rangers had, singlehanded, arrested a wanted man
by the name of Jacob "Stormy" Stoermer. Brought him

into Palestine with his hands cuffed behind him, his feet tied together under his horse's belly—this after Stormy had vowed never to be taken alive.

A fool doctor insisted that Stormy be untied when he complained of stomach pains. When Stormy broke loose, armed himself, and fled the town, it was Lieutenant Oaks who went after him and brought him back. This time, Stormy came in tied across his saddle, dead.

Stormy was supposed to have $6300 in currency on him, loot from the robbery of a Southern Pacific train, the first time he was arrested. When he broke loose in the doctor's office, Lieutenant Oaks was just counting out the money to his superior officer, Captain Giles Crawford. It checked out to the dime.

A week after Stormy's death, he was identified as the man who had held up a poker game in Corsicana, taking $285 in currency. There had been no time for him to spend any of it before Casey Oaks ran him down a second time, and killed him.

By the time the Corsicana robbery story came out, Lieutenant Oaks and his wife were on their way to El Paso to a new assignment. Casey's captaincy was on the Governor's desk for signature. There had not been a cent on Stormy's body. Captain (now Colonel) Crawford recovered two brand-new ten-dollar bills that had been taken in the Corsicana robbery.

He got them from the railroad, which had taken

them in from Lieutenant Oaks to pay for his train tickets to El Paso. Arriving in El Paso, Casey found not a new job and a promotion but a telegraphic warrant for his own arrest. He resigned without ever admitting that he had taken the money.

He was never prosecuted. Neither had he ever been forgiven for compromising the honor of the Rangers for a miserable $285.

A weaker man would have been destroyed, but Casey settled down and ran for sheriff. He was quickly a power to be reckoned with in that part of southwest Texas. To his natural craftiness and strength of character, the senator thought, there had been added the implacability of the fanatic. Casey had changed since the death of his wife. He would pull the temple down, to have his way.

"I'm not your judge, Case," the senator said. "You took that money. That's the way things was done in them days. I'll tell the Governor he had better learn to live with facts and find you some kind of a job."

"Ferris Terry's job," the sheriff growled.

"No, no." Chidester shook his head. "That job requires a bond and an examination of your record. It would bring Colonel Crawford, commander of the Texas Rangers, into it. And not even the Governor can handle him. Case, Crawford is a lunatic!"

The sheriff settled back comfortably in his chair,

smiling a humorless smile under his sweeping mustache. "So am I," he said. "You tell the Governor that, Aub. Tell him I have went *loco* out here. Just *loco* enough to elect Mike Banterman to Congress."

CHAPTER FIVE

Where Raitt squatted with the rifle across his lap, the cold wind could not reach him but the warm sun could. The rock at his back had been warmed all morning by the sun. His hat, and the denim jacket given to him by the Bar M cook, were off so the heat from the rock could warm his back. He had eaten well this morning, and lacked only two things for comfort—sleep, and a drink.

He had not dared sleep around Eph Crippen. He could keep Eph nerved to his work by sheer force, the gift of command that a man like himself had over riffraff like Eph. Let him sleep, though, and the kid was a cinch to try to get his rifle back.

The need for a drink had come on suddenly as he squatted here. He staved it off by running a series of entrancing thoughts through his mind. The wealth and warmth of Hermosillo. Hatred of bastards like Mike Banterman and Bru Hawley. The money.

The money, the money, the money—above all, the money that would get them to Hermosillo in style. Get a house down there with trees for a hammock, and flowers. Get one of those little Indian girls Bru talked about, a real young one. Get—

A sharp whistle came to his ears. He clamped his hat on and turned, tilting to his knees with the rifle under his arm. Down there in the gully, beside the wagon road, Eph Crippen was shouting something. Raitt waved to him.

"Come up here! I can't hear a word you say."

Elbows and knees flying awkwardly, Eph loped up the slope. "Somebody's coming in a rig of some kind," he panted. "I think it's Mike and somebody else."

"A rig? What kind?" Raitt said sharply.

"Buggy or spring wagon. It sure ain't no heavy freight wagon."

Raitt straightened his mustache nervously with the back of his hand. "Tell you what. Go back down there and watch them. Unless it's somebody like the sheriff, somebody like that, you come flopping out at the last minute like we planned."

"Like I was hurt," Eph said.

"Yes, pretty bad. You can't walk or talk. You—"

"My horse throwed me and run off."

Raitt said impatiently, "Just stop them, and then don't get between them and me, you hear now? Take their guns when I tell you to, but not before!"

Eph was excited, but he could take orders. He

nodded solemnly. "Then tie them up afterward. That's all I got to do."

Raitt made a smile. "No, then you've got to get us to Hermosillo. Better get going, Eph."

Eph loped back down the slope and crouched beside the wagon road. There were several kinds of white trash, Raitt thought. Mike Banterman was a pushy money-maker, no respect for anything. Depend on a man like him, say a blacksmith or a bootmaker, and pretty soon he owned half of your land.

Bru Hawley was another kind, hardworking and silent, dangerous only if you insisted that he keep his almost-white place. Eph Crippen was still another kind, a transplanted hillbilly whose pale eyes and hair and possum sharpness of face meant that, in his ancestry, too many cousins had bred cousins. Brothers and sisters, too, if all you heard about those people was true.

People like Eph were unclean animals, sly and treacherous and temperish. Yet they lived with arms, and their suspicion of outsiders had made them good soldiers. They could not be driven. But they could be led.

Kneeling there beside the rock, waiting for the rig to come in sight, Raitt ran his palm across his face and brought it away dry despite the feeling of being sweaty. Only a drinking man could know about these dry fits. Soon he'd get short of breath. His stomach

would go into spasms. If he did not get a drink then—
or if something did not distract him in time—he was in
danger of going into a screaming convulsion.

Something distracted him. The rig came in sight,
a good team trotting along smartly. Raitt's nerves
stopped singing. His vision cleared as he recognized
Mike Banterman and the man who sat beside him, driving the team.

Woody Brown, the nigra foreman!

Behind the two men, something big and bulky but
light in weight was tied into the wagon with taut ropes.
It made a perfect backdrop, against which the two
men were silhouetted sharply. The fit might come on
Raitt again, but for the moment he was steady as a rock.
He lifted the big rifle, slipped the safety, and held it
ready to put across the rock.

He did not dare look out until Eph had caught their
attention and stopped them. He heard the trace chains
and neckyoke hardware jingle as the team shied suddenly.

"Why, dog my soul, hit's the Crippen boy!" came
Woody Brown's voice. "He's been hurt, Mike."

"Well, see to him!" Mike shouted.

Raitt slid the rifle up over the rock and dared a look.
Eph had come flopping out into the middle of the road,
overacting, making an emergency out of a plan
already tight. Those two were not fools.

"Ah, ah, ah!" Eph gurgled.

"Hol' the team, Mike," said Woody. "I got to see what ail dis boy."

Raitt pushed his hat back and let it fall behind him. He waited until Mike had taken the lines and the Negro had turned to descend by the right front wheel.

He pressed the trigger with a light, professional contraction of his whole hand. The big gun thudded back against his shoulder. Raitt, holding his breath for the shot, tasted the acrid gun smoke on his tongue.

Woody Brown's entire head disintegrated. His huge body cartwheeled, hit inertly, as Raitt shifted the gun and clacked the heavy bolt. A hot brass empty flew out, and another slug slid into the chamber on greased lands.

He centered on Mike Banterman's chest, squeezed off one more, and clacked the bolt to jack another shell into the chamber. He did not need it.

"In the heart, by God!" Raitt said as he stood up. He waved his hat at Eph. "Stop the team, Eph. Catch them, you fool!"

Mike's head struck the doubletrees. He kept on falling and came down on the wagon tongue, between the horses. Raitt began running as the team bolted.

Eph had to jump for the bits to save his own life. Mike Banterman's body broke loose and fell to the ground. The team went up in the air, lifting Eph with them. He screamed in terror.

"Mr. Raitt, Mr. Raitt, I can't hold them!"

The crazed team was a hundred feet off the road when Raitt, carrying the .45-70, caught the back endgate of the wagon. It was a dresser and a bedstead tied in the wagon box. He went over them and caught the lines with both hands, holding the rifle between his knees.

"Jump! Let go, Eph. I've got them!"

Eph sprawled out of the way. Raitt ran the team off the road and took them in a wide circle across gullies and up slopes. He took his chances on overturning, and while it lasted, he showed that pale-eyed hillbilly brat how a horseman handled a horse.

"Ho, ho—ho now!"

When he got them stopped, he was back on the road, a hundred yards back of where Eph's play-acting had stopped them. Eph staggered over to stand between the bodies of the two dead men.

"Jesus, you didn't need to kill them!"

"Yes, I did," said Raitt.

"You never did mean to just hold them up! You lied to me!" Eph screamed.

"You goddam right! Eph, you can't hold up folks you know. It's a personal thing, then. He'll take his chances with you. You're too green to know that, but I'm not. One of them would've killed you."

For the first time, Eph dared to look him in the eye. "That ain't why you killed them!"

"No, it ain't," Raitt said, smiling. "Go ahead and take your chances, boy, if you feel like it. If I kill you, it'll be because I have to. But I will, and you know I will."

He saw the insane fear in the hillbilly's eyes. He saw it go away, too. Nobody wanted to become Number Three, but these hillbillies were tetched about arms.

"With my own goddam rifle! Onliest gun I ever owned, and the first thing it kills is Mr. Banterman."

"No, the nigra was first. Hush up, Eph, and help me. This team won't stand."

"Stand where?"

"For Christ's sake, come hold them!"

The kid could take orders, yes he could. He took the bit of one horse, and held it while Raitt got down. Carrying the rifle in his left hand, Raitt shot the two horses with his .45.

He made Eph help him rob the bodies of the dead men—not because he needed help, but to teach Eph how far he was into this business. All the way! The money was in a leather purse in Mike's hip pocket. It was all brand-new gold, fresh from the mint—$380.

Ten gold eagles and fourteen double eagles, all marked 1886, with 1887 almost four months away.

"We struck it rich, kid," Raitt said with a thoughtful scowl. There was an old gambler's saying: new money is new luck. What did it suggest?

In Woody's pocket they found another new double eagle, plus $14.80 in bills and silver. There was also a receipted bill for one dresser and one bedstead.

"Here's what happened, Eph," Raitt said. "Old man paid him forty dollars, two double eagles. He paid some bills and bought this cheap furniture, like a good nigra. This is what's left. Well, he ain't going to get no sleep on this bed, is he?"

"You going to burn it, Mr. Raitt?"

"And send up smoke you can see for ten miles? You just listen and learn, boy. Unless somebody blunders along, it'll be tomorrow before this is found," Raitt said.

"Then put yourself in their place. Here's two dead men and two dead horses. Who was shot first, the men or the horses? Why was the team run around in a circle like that? Why's the men here, and the horses back there? It'll take hours to figger it out!"

"That old sheriff, he ain't no fool. Used to be a Texas Ranger until he got into some kind of trouble."

"Sho'! But it'll take a spell to do it. Every track we made, we're going to wipe out now. Then we go right back down the road and we skin around town and head for the Rio. We'll be halfway to Hermosillo before they even find these dead men."

Eph squinted at him almost pitifully. "Don't it bother you none that you shot them, Mr. Raitt? It would me."

Raitt's strong, bony hand closed on the youth's shoulder. "You shot them as much as me. It was your gun. You baited them to stop so I could shoot them. How you figger I'm in any deeper than you are?"

It would take the kid a while to get used to being a murderer, but get used to it he would, because get used to it he must. Meanwhile he stumbled as he walked. His pale eyes were full of grief—not for Mike Banterman and Woody Brown, but for his lost innocence. For the time when he had been merely worthless, not a murderer.

Raitt carried the rifle to where their horses were tied, nearly half a mile away. Eph, who had been so jealous of the rifle, now did not even look at it. With his pocket knife, Raitt cut two big pieces of brush, which they dragged behind them to wipe out their tracks and those of the horses.

"Cain't hide them entirely," Raitt said, "but the more you give them to play Injun with, the more you slow them down. You got to waste their time, see?"

"I reckon you learned this in the war."

"Well, I should say so!" Raitt's burning need for a

drink was gone. He felt calm, almost elated, and fit for anything. "It was hell while it lasted, but I'll tell you this, Eph. My generation is a hell of a lot tougher than yours, because of it. I can take care of you like you never could take care of me, because I was an officer, a captain."

"I be dad-blamed. A captain!"

"Yes, sir. I'm an old man now, but I was a captain of cavalry. Dragoons, we called them, when I joined up. Night raids, Eph, were our specialty. Troop I commanded made sixteen night raids, pistol and saber, ride over them and ride out, you see. That's how we got fresh mounts, kid! Took them from the blue-bellies."

Nice to be able to talk this way. Long years ago, Raitt had learned to talk less than freely about his part in the war. Every now and then some jay bird insisted on knowing what your regiment was—and Raitt's had been a thing called the Governor's House Guards.

Formed up behind the Governor—for parades, speeches, and hospital visits. Dress grays for weddings at the Mansion, opening of the Legislature, or for guard of honor when President Davis came to town.

Like that. Old veterans of the Indian wars, young men with consumption, missing fingers, or perhaps just hollow hearts. Toward the last, the scarlet facings on the dress grays turned yellow-pink. The horses got worse, and there were no promotions. And afterward, no brevet ranks, as was the case with the victors.

And not captain. Lieutenant. Nor had Raitt served in Virginia. That was why that derisive nickname, "Tidewater," had made him squirm so. It was an old sore place that would not heal. It was one of the reasons that Mike Banterman now was dead.

CHAPTER SIX

"This job is good for your soul," said Clyde Fox with an arch grin that showed he expected appropriate laughter. "It learns you to be meek and humble."

"If it don't, nothing will," Bru Hawley said.

The two were hauling fresh horse manure and bedding straw, and piling it against the north side of the house. It was something new to Bru, but it made sense once Woody explained it to him. It kept the winter wind out from under the foundations, and it did not freeze, the way dirt would.

"I reckon we's teacher's pets," Clyde said. "Woody, like the Lord, chastiseth whom He loves."

Bru looked up at the sun. "Mr. Banterman and Woody are late."

"Yes. Something must've come up."

"Maybe he changed his mind about giving us tomorrow off."

"No, Mike wouldn't do that."

A door in the house slammed. Mrs. Banterman and the old kitchen maid, Socorra, came carrying a big pail between them. "Better pack this on down to the hogs, before the dogs upset it," the rancher's wife said.

"Yes'm, right away, ma'am," said Clyde.

The woman looked up at the sun. "I wonder what's keeping Mike? It's long past noon. I thought he'd be back before this."

"So did I, ma'am. We was just saying that."

She did not reply. The two women returned to the house. Clyde leaned on his pitchfork to watch them out of sight. "Mm, *mmm!*" he said softly. "Mike takes to staying away from home too long, that's one of the chores I'd be proud to take on for him."

Bru leaned on his pitchfork too. "I don't care to hear a woman talked about that way, and I don't reckon Mr. Banterman would either."

"Oh, pshaw, a man can look, can't he? Mike's an old man. How can he take care of that by hisself? Woman like that is like a horse. She's got to be worked out regular or she gets out of hand. I'd do Mike a favor to take her for a canter once in a while."

"You know what?" Bru said. "You're just a plain damn fool, talking that way."

Clyde grinned his foolish grin again, picked up the kitchen slop pail, and walked away with it. The bunk-house joker, Bru thought, watching him go. Mr. Banterman's pet clown, and one day he'll go too far and get his fool head shot off. . . . He had known too many like Fox. Dodge a lot of the hard work by cuddling up to the boss, but always the first to double-cross him.

Mr. Banterman's absence worried Bru somehow, far more than it should have. Mike had gone out of his way to be cordial to Bru, to show him he did not hold his association with Eldon Raitt against him. He seemed to be the kind of man who leaned over backward to be fair. To be dilatory in keeping a promise to his whole crew was out of character.

No one had gone out to rake the far brush for stray cattle today. Every man's horse stood saddled. Every man was shaved. The cook had fed them before noon. The men were finding make-work jobs around the place, counting the minutes until Mike got back.

Clyde returned with the empty slop pail. The kitchen maid opened the door to take it in. Bru spoke to her in Spanish. She looked a little startled, but she replied at some length in the same language.

"You talk that Mexican lingo as good as she does," Clyde said when the woman had gone inside with the pail. "What'd she say?"

"She's mighty worried that Mr. Banterman ain't back. She thinks somebody ort to go look for him."

Clyde picked up his pitchfork, held it irresolutely a

moment, and then drove it into the ground. "Come on! Let somebody put this team up, and let's you and me go look for Mike."

"You kind of take charge, don't you?"

"Do as you please."

"I'll go with you, but I think we better ask Mrs. Banterman first."

He went to the kitchen door and knocked. When Socorra answered, he asked her, in Spanish, to speak to *la Señora*. The rancher's wife came to the door.

"What's the trouble?" she said.

"None that I know of, ma'am," Bru said, holding his hat in his hand, "but Clyde and me thought we'd head for town and see if maybe they haven't busted down somewhere."

"It's certainly not like him to be so late."

Not the prettiest woman I ever seen, Bru thought, but surely the nicest. . . . "That's what the boys say, ma'am. They could bust a wheel easy on that road, or a reach or hame strap or something."

"It's a new wagon and new harness, but anything can happen. Let me know if you find out anything, please."

"You bet, ma'am."

The door closed on her. Deep South, by her speech, with the kind of manners Raitt was always talking about. Raitt talked a lot about the women of the South, but it took one like Mrs. Banterman to show how little Raitt really knew about them.

Bru let Clyde pick out horses for them. In ten minutes they were on their way, munching sandwiches the cook had supplied for them. They let the two big, powerful geldings run.

In two hours, only one exchange of conversation took place between them.

"Some warmer today," Bru said.

"Yes, and it's mighty curious that Mike would waste maybe the last good weekend," Clyde replied.

"You don't like the looks of this, do you?"

"I don't, and that's a fact. We should've met them long before now."

Shortly they saw buzzards circling a spot on the road ahead of them, where it dipped through the brushy gullies Bru remembered from that first ride out here. He looked at Clyde, and was puzzled by the pallid, frozen expression on his face. It was more than worry. It was downright fear.

S'pose, Bru thought, it's a dead horse. Maybe they had a runaway. But where's the other horse, and where are they? They all killed in one runaway? I reckon it could happen, but . . .

When they reached the dead men and the dead

horses, buzzards were already tearing at the wound in one of the horses. Screaming curses, Clyde tumbled from the saddle and flapped his hat at them.

"Hold up!" Bru shouted, as the buzzards took wing. "Don't foul the sign."

He dismounted. The two stood there, staring at the dead men. Bru knelt down and touched Mike Banterman's neck. His face had been smashed badly, but there was no mistake about who it was.

"They ain't been dead too long," he said, looking up at Clyde. "No more than an hour."

"I didn't do this. I didn't have nothing to do with it," Clyde said.

Bru stood up and walked toward him. "Why would anybody think you did?"

"Well, Woody too—they killed him too—you was with me all morning—you *know* it wasn't me!"

The time to get it out of him was now, before he got his wits back. Bru dropped his horse's reins and drove his fist into Clyde's stomach, knocking him back against his own horse. Clyde's mouth came open. He clutched at his stomach with both arms and slumped to his knees, paralyzed by the punch in the solar plexus.

Bru took off his hat and slapped Clyde across the face with it, again and again. He knew when the paralysis left Clyde and he got his breath back. Bru pulled his gun out and hit Clyde across the side of the face with the flat of it. He raised it to jab him in the forehead with the butt.

"Start talking, you son of a bitch, or I'll split your goddam head wide open! What has Woody got to do with it? Last chance, boy—"

It took some time to get the story straight. Week or ten days ago, Clyde had made some remark about Mrs. Banterman, in front of Woody Brown. It was not the first time, but it was probably the rawest remark he had ever dared. Woody had picked him up by the neck in both big hands, and simply squeezed.

When Clyde came to, he was lying on his face on the ground. His whole body ached. All he could see was Woody's big feet. When he rolled over, slowly and carefully, he could see Woody shaving strips of cut plug for his pipe.

"You beat up on me!" Clyde sobbed.

"I pawed you around a little, yes I did."

"You ain't got no right to lay your goddam hands on me!"

"I taken the right," Woody said. "I ain't fightin' Mike's battles, no *sir!* This was purely on my own bill. I don't like to hear *no* woman made light of. If it was Mike, he'd take this and make a steer of you. Mind yo' manners, boy, you goin' work fo' me."

That was all. "I don't mind working for him," Clyde said, "but he ain't going to lay his goddam black hands on me. But you know I didn't have nothing to do with this!"

The methodical ferocity of the killings brought Eldon Raitt vividly to Bru's mind. He said, "No, you didn't. You's with me all morning."

"He waved that knife at me. He—"

"Shut up! Somebody's got to flog it into town and stir out the sheriff. Somebody's got to stay here and guard these bodies."

"Somebody's got to tell Mrs. Banterman, too."

"That's the sheriff's job! Goddam it, forget that woman! What's this sheriff's name?"

"Casey Oaks."

"Is he any good?"

"He's a tough old son of a bitch. They say he stoled some money once and got drummed out of the Rangers. I don't think I want to face him, way I feel."

"I'll go get him. You stay here, and don't let them stinking birds touch these bodies! Listen, there's that furniture in the wagon, and a horse blanket. Let's cover them up with the blanket and the mattress from the bed."

"Why?"

I don't know why, Bru thought, except that I don't trust you worth a damn. . . . They covered the bodies without disturbing them. Clyde's horse had started back toward the Bar M. After catching his own, Bru had to run Clyde's horse down before starting to town.

Well, he thought as he rode, I'm in a pack of trouble now. If Eldon Raitt done this, I'm in such trouble as I never been in before. . . .

He tried to remember Raitt, first impressions as well as last ones. A kind of bossy charm, a way of looking at you like you might not be in his class but he liked you anyway. His queer, sarcastic, drawling comments kept you grinning.

The charm wore off fast when you found out he was a three-times-a-year drunk. Raitt's fault they were deadfalled and robbed in El Paso. The fool was all in favor of going back and killing the bartender. That would have had the whole town down on them. There was a time to show fight and a time to swallow your lumps and ride on, and Raitt had no judgment.

It was dark when he reached town. The first person he saw was a tall man in a neat gray tailcoat, with a ruffled scarf about his neck and a well-brushed white hat. Bru reined in beside him.

"Where's the sheriff's office, sir?" he said.

"Yonder, in the cellar of the courthouse," the man said, "but he won't be there at this hour. I'm on my way to his house, if you want to follow me."

"No time, sir. There's been a murder."

"Then don't let me keep you. Turn yander, and it's the last house on the street."

Bru touched his hat and prodded his tired horse into a run. The sheriff was carrying in his evening pail of milk, a chore he did not know how to get rid of in his widowhood. He did not even know what to do with the milk his cow gave. He did not know, in fact, what to do with his life, with Blanche dead.

He listened without a change of expression to Bru's story. "I don't know you," he said at the end. "You must be a new man out there."

"Yes I am, sheriff."

"You hired out with that Tidewater fella?"

"Yes. You know anything about him?"

"Only what Mike said. Clyde Fox is with the bodies?"

"Yes."

"Mighty odd, the two of you."

"What about the two of us?"

"The one that rode in with that Tidewater man, and the one making eyes at Mike's wife. By God, what a pair to find the bodies!"

Bru said stridently, "We found them because we looked for them. Everybody at the Bar M can tell you we never left the place all day. If this is all you aim to do about it, I'll tell it to your face—you're a piss-poor specimen of a sheriff!"

The man who had directed Bru to the house came hurrying up the sidewalk. "Understand you've got a killing on your hands, Case, so I won't keep you," he said. "I believe I'll hire a rig to take me to the rails and catch the night train to Austin. I'll see the Governor first thing tomorrow."

"Don't hurry on my account, Aubrey," the sheriff said. "It was Mike Banterman that was murdered."

It took only a few minutes to collect a posse, fill lanterns, and load guns they were unlikely to use. When they reached the scene, the covered bodies were still undefiled. But there was no sign of Clyde Fox.

CHAPTER SEVEN

The clock had run down before noon. It was Mike's job to wind it, but he was careless about details and this was not the first time it had stopped. She had no good idea what time it was.

"*¿Señora?*" came a diffident voice.

Velma was sitting on the edge of the bed, darning socks. She looked around and saw Socorra in the door. "*¿Mande?*" she said.

It was one of the few Spanish words she knew, and she could not make out Socorra's reply. Something about the cowboys—*vaqueros*. She recognized that word. She put her darning down and followed Socorra to the back door. At least half the gang stood beside their saddled horses just beyond the fence.

"What's the trouble, boys?" she said. Mike always addressed them as "boys."

One of the old, white-haired crips that Mike kept on to do chores around the place appointed himself spokesman. "Mike was supposed to be back by noon, ma'am," he said. "We wanted him to wait and go in with us, and pay us in town. No, he had to go fetch the money back. It just ain't fair, ma'am, after he promised."

"Why isn't it fair?"

"Why, there ain't more than a few hours of daylight left, Mrs. Banterman. We supposed to work all day and then ride into town in the dark? That ain't what I call taking the day off, ma'am."

They had not worked all day, not by any means, but she felt a sudden pang of disquiet. "Woody was with Mike. I'm sure he'll be back soon."

"That's what's worrying us. I don't hardly see how the both of them could've had a runaway."

"Do you want to go look for them?"

"All of us?"

Her nerves were suddenly screaming, for some reason. "No, somebody should stay here, for God's sake! The two boys that Woody had banking the house left some time ago. Go help them, in case anything's wrong, but let me know the minute you know anything."

She watched them ride out, raising a tall cloud of dust in the chill air. As Velma returned to the house, she passed Socorra. The maid said something—quite a lot of something. Velma understood just enough to realize that the maid thought it was high time the men had gone looking for Mike and Woody.

Darkness came much too soon. The cook's helper

did the milking, and brought the milk to the house. Socorra strained it into crocks and set it out on the screened porch, to chill and stay sweet. She skimmed the cream from the morning milk and poured the skimmed milk into the pail for the hogs.

Have to put a stop to that waste, Velma thought. Make cottage cheese a couple of times a week. Mike never ate it before we were married, and he loves it. . . .

They lighted only the kitchen lamps, plus the one in the front window that was kept lighted for strangers who blundered into the place. She ate in the kitchen with the maids.

The first she knew that the men had returned was when she heard a man's deep voice baying orders in the back yard: "Get me all the lanterns you can, and be sure they're full of coal oil. Hook up two teams, and put some blankets in the wagon bed. Jump to it! You run around like a bunch of God-danged old hens."

That sounded like Sheriff Oaks. She hurried to the back door, snatching a lantern from the hands of one of the maids. She met the sheriff coming up the path from the bunkhouse.

"Oh, hello, Casey!" she said. "Have you seen anything of Mike and Woody?"

The sheriff put his own lantern down and reached

for hers. He locked both of her hands into one of his and said, "Take a tuck in yourself, Velma. I got to belt you a hard one right in the belly."

She reeled on her feet, feeling the ice come down over her. "Oh, my God, he's dead!" she whimpered.

"Yes," he said hoarsely, "and Woody, too. Poor little Dolores, you're going to have to help her and them kids over the hump. You're the *Señora* here now. That's going to be part of your job."

One at a time, she took command of her weak, treacherous joints. She stood erect and did not shed a tear. "What happened?" she said calmly.

Meanwhile she was thinking, Why, I'm really Texicated, as Mike used to say. Taking this like a Texas wife. Worrying about that black man's little widow instead of making a scene. I taught Mike a lot. But, oh, he taught me some things, too . . . !

Casey told her about it in a spooky voice. He could hardly believe what he had seen. He walked with her past the weeping maids, and Socorra shoved the coffee pot to the front of the stove and put in some fat pitchwood to make a quick fire. They sat down together, and he tried to tell her about it without hurting her too much.

"I'll have to wait for daylight to try to work out the sign, but it was some kind of a rifle. A *big* rifle! Two men, and they tried to wipe out their trails afterward and didn't do too good a job, so fur as I can tell. Their pockets was picked, but this wasn't no ordinary road-agent job."

"What makes you think that? Mike was supposed to have a lot of money on him."

"This was assassination. It was somebody they knowed, that they could testify to later. Who in the name of God would just gun Mike and Woody down like that?"

"Almost anybody. Mike didn't preach love-thy-neighbor. He said what he thought, and you never know how people take things. But the nerve—that's something else. I can't think of anyone who could do it!"

"I can. Now, lady, you've got to let Dolores know. I can do it, but you're the *Señora*. You'll have to be with me."

She stood up calmly. "I'll tell her, but you come along. Dolores speaks English. Just go with me; that's all I ask."

The black man's Mexican wife—widow, now—took it very well indeed. She gathered her four children around her under the Sacred Heart in the corner, where she kept a candle burning. There she prayed for the soul of the black giant who had married her in her own church while remaining faithful himself to the Arise Baptists.

"Where will you bury the *Señor?*" she asked afterward.

"Why, here, of course," said Velma. "Why?"

"I don't know where to bury Woody."

"Here! Where else would you bury him? This was his home, Dolores. He will lie near Mike, if you'll let him."

"A black man, *Señora?*"

"I don't like that kind of talk, Dolores," she said sternly. "Woody was my husband's friend."

Finally Dolores could cry. Velma and Casey walked back to the house together. "That's the way to handle her," the sheriff grunted. "The way Mike would do things is going to be the right way for you, in case you ever have any doubts, Velma."

"I have many."

"I suppose you know Mike's will by heart?"

"No idea."

"Everything is yours. He was just talking about it today. I was the one held him in town so late, you know. He kept saying he had to be home by noon, but I held him there talking."

"About what?"

"I wanted him to run for Congress. I still think it was a good idee."

She nodded. "He would have had a lot to learn, but he would have been so good at it! He was a learner."

"You're a pair of learners. I never seen the beat of how you taken holt here, Velma."

"I hardly know myself. Nothing in the way I was brought up prepared me for any of the things I have had to do here. Yet I did live up to Mike, didn't I?"

"And then some."

"Oh, Casey, I'll miss him so much! I can't go on living up to him if he's not here."

"Yes you can," he said harshly. "You think you can't, but when the time comes, you'll find there's no way to let go. Ain't many things I can advise you on, Velma, but that's one of them."

He was back at the scene by dawn, driving one fast, steady team on a box wagon and leading another to pull the spring wagon home. With him was one of Mike's Mexican riders—nephew of Socorra, cousin of Dolores, and crafty old tracker who had learned from the Comanches. They went over the sign together.

"Here one sat with the rifle, Casey, behind this rock. Yonder waited the other, beside the road."

"Why? What was he doing down there?"

The Mexican shrugged. "To make them look at him, while this one shot him. What else?"

"Where are the empty shells?"

"He picked them up and took them with him. A

gun so big, to smash Woody's head—the shells cost much, eh? It was a very big rifle, Casey. Very big!"

"What kind? Who owns such a gun?"

"Who knows? One hears of the Springfield. A .45-caliber bullet, seventy grains of powder. But it may be a rifle I never heard of, Casey."

"And then straight to Mexico."

"Not through town, certainly. Even now, they are riding like hell toward the river, I think."

The sheriff rubbed his tired eyes thoughtfully. "I think I know the one who set here and done the shooting. Know who he was, anyway. But the other man, who was he?"

"Who knows? Maybe somebody that Mike or Woody knew. For somebody they knew, they would stop and not be—you know, watchful and afraid."

"I reckon. We'll look for a lean, gray-haired Tidewater man with a .45-70 Springfield, and somebody that knowed Mike and Woody well enough so's they wouldn't suspicion him. But where the hell we'll look, I sure don't know."

The kid who had ridden into town to tell him about the murder came up to where the sheriff leaned wearily against the ambush rock, beside the tracker. "How long you fixing to wait around here, sheriff?" he said. "Time we got these bodies home."

"Let's see, your name is Hawley, Brutus Hawley, you say."

"Yes, if that matters."

"You kind of take command, don't you, Hawley?"

"It's time somebody did. The bastards that done this ain't going to hang around here to swap chewing tobacco with you, and these men have got to be buried."

"You take them back and see that they get a decent burial. Tell Mrs. Banterman I'm sorry I can't be there, but I've got work to do. One thing, kid."

Hawley did not change expression as the sheriff jabbed him in the chest with his forefinger. He towered over Hawley by half a head, but somehow the kid gave the impression of meeting him eye to eye.

"Mike never had no foreman but Woody. Mrs. Banterman has got nobody she can depend on out there. You's so damn free with idees, see if you can't make yourself useful to her. Keep this gang of his busy! Ride their tails, get as many cows branded as you can before snow flies. I reckon you know who I think done this."

"Eldon Raitt."

"That's my guess."

"Mine too." Hawley's eyes narrowed slightly. "You better not be saying I had anything to do with it."

"If I ever say that, you won't have no way of misunderstanding it. You let me worry about Eldon Raitt.

You just make yourself useful to that poor woman out there at the Bar M."

The sheriff started for town the moment the wagons were on their way toward the Bar M.

He was almost into town when he met riders bearing fresh bad news. The Porter & Beeson State Bank had been robbed that morning, of $4800, all in new ten-dollar and twenty-dollar gold pieces.

The robbers had taken Eli Porter from his house just before daylight, forced him to open the bank and vault, and then had left him tied and gagged under his own office table. Two men, Eli said. He had not seen one of them at all, had not even heard his voice. All he knew was that the bandit boss had given soft orders to someone, and they had been obeyed.

He had seen the bandit leader clearly. A soft-talking Southerner, with heavy gray eyebrows above a mask of faded gray gingham like a rag torn from a woman's old dress. A thin man, almost gaunt, wearing an old denim jacket over a thin, worn, faded shirt. He wore a .45 pistol, and carried a Springfield .45-70 rifle.

CHAPTER EIGHT

The fire had gone out, but Raitt was in a keyed-up state in which he did not feel cold, tired, or hungry. A man got only one chance this big in life, and his time was here. What did newly minted gold coin signify? To some gamblers, it meant luck. To Raitt, it meant a *shipment* of money.

Where this had come from, there would be more. He put out the toe of his boot to prod Eph, who was curled up asleep beside the dead fire. It had taken Eph a long time to go to sleep. His pea brain, dulled by remorse, by yesterday's horror, had had room for only one thought: his precious Springfield .45-70. Grab it and be gone, before anything worse happened.

But Eph had slept, and Raitt had not. He jogged Eph harder. "Wake up, kid! Let's ride," he said.

Eph came back to dismal reality reluctantly. He staggered to his feet, his eyes falling at once on the new rifle. His face fell when he saw it across Raitt's lap, out of reach.

"This banker," Raitt said. "What if he has moved? You been gone from town a right smart spell."

"Where would he move to?" Eph said dully, scratching himself. "He's got the nicest house in town."

"Saddle up, then."

"Why don't you saddle up?"

"Because I'm wide awake, and you're not. And because I give the orders, Eph."

"You act like I work for you."

Raitt showed his fine teeth in a genial smile. "You do, but I work for you too. I declare, if you ain't the worst boy to argue! Now go saddle up."

One thing sure, he thought, as they rode quietly into town a few minutes later, we've got to get rid of this kid's horse. . . . The pinto was so conspicuous it put his teeth on edge. A second-rate horse, too, and it would be remembered wherever they rode it.

"Here's the place to tie," Eph said shrilly. He was getting nervous again. "Nobody ever goes through these willers."

"Sho', this will do just fine!"

They dismounted, led their horses back into the dense willow brush, and tied them.

"You ain't going to kill him now, are you?" Eph said piteously.

"I told you I wouldn't. Don't you fret! We'll just take his money and sashay on."

Daylight was minutes away as they walked the path through the willows. Suddenly, where the willows ended, a tall yellow house loomed. There was a white rail fence around it, a boxed well with a long white sweep beside it, and a porch whose railing was gripped stoutly by a teeming rat's nest of dry honeysuckle vines.

Raitt studied it carefully, pleased at what he saw. If Eph was right, this banker got up at five-thirty every morning and made himself a pot of coffee. That hour could not be far off.

"Lay down next to the fence, yonder," Raitt whispered. "When I get my gun on him, I'll hold him so you can duck into the willers before he sees your face. But don't start nothing until I tell you 'Now!'"

"You're going to kill him," Eph whimpered.

"No. Now buck up, boy! You're doing just fine. Go lay down there, and stay hid."

Eph stumbled over to the fence and lay down in the high, dry weeds there. He was completely invisible. Raitt squatted at the corner of the house, on his toes, leaning forward against the rifle. He was just beginning to feel the cold when he heard a noise inside the house.

He looked up. A yellow glow passed a window—the banker, carrying a lamp! The glow vanished toward the kitchen, in the back of the house. Raitt cupped his hands around his mouth.

"Eph, now!" he called softly.

Given something he could do—perhaps the one

thing in the world he did well—Eph performed almost too well. His imitation of two tomcats fighting was so lifelike that it was creepy. An old one and a young one, taking their misery out on each other after a lonely and disappointing night.

You could almost see it. They closed with a shriek. A howl of agony from the young one, as they sprang apart. Now they circled each other, growling. They closed again. A low-pitched, grumbling noise, as the young tom worked on the old one's throat.

Then a squawl of agony, as the old one walked his long hind claws against the young one's soft belly. It was kind of pitiful, about Eph. A man who could imitate a cat fight was not much in demand.

The door opened. A man stepped out in pants, slippers, and dressing gown. "You pesky cats!" he said. "Begone. Shut up there. Scat, scat, scat!"

Raitt stood up, leaned over the railing, and shuffled the muzzle of the rifle through the opening in the front of the banker's dressing gown. The gown fell open, exposing the banker in his nightshirt.

"Keep quiet and you're all right, sir," Raitt said softly. "This thing could cut you in two. Now reach behind you, careful, and close the door. Then you and me is going to walk to the bank."

The old man's pouched eyes were riveted on the big

rifle. "You have got the aces on me," he said. "Just tell me what to do, and I'll sure do it."

"That's fine, Mr. Porter. We'll walk the back path to the bank, just like always."

"Is this a stick-up? You can't get away with it. I can't open the vault by myself, and there ain't much in it if I could."

Raitt did not mind a little talk, to give Eph a chance to snake back into the willows, but enough was enough. "I do hope we ain't going to disagree on that, sir. Shape I'm in, either I get that money, or I'm forced to kill you deader than hell."

"Maybe I can help you. How much do you need, cowboy? A little loan is better than—"

"You get walking, Mr. Porter. Move!"

He steered the banker with the rifle. He knew when Eph Crippen dropped in behind them. The banker's own feet had worn this short-cut path. When they came out the willows on the other side, they were on a small hitching lot behind the bank. Not a light was visible anywhere in town. Not a sound was to be heard—not even an early rooster or a stray dog.

The bank was an old, squat building of stone masonry. Neither Raitt nor Eph had ever been inside it. "We'll go in the back door, Mr. Porter," Raitt said as they approached it. "We won't need any lights in there, will we? And no reaching for guns, either. I don't know where they are, but you just reach out for anything and I cut you in two, right across the back-bone."

"What worries me," Porter quavered, "is that we're just a little old cow-town bank. I can't give you what ain't here."

"You's so worried, I think you got something in there to worry about. Open up now, sir."

Porter took the keys from his pocket and unlocked the bank door. Raitt pushed him inside with the .45-70. "Wait a minute now," he whispered. "You know your way, sir, but I have to get used to the dark."

They waited a moment. He heard Eph come up behind them, breathing hard from sheer nerves. "Going just fine," he said, over his shoulder. "Close the door behind us, stay out of sight, and you just wait."

Raitt jiggled the gun against the banker's back. "Let's go open your safe now, sir."

"It takes two of us. Two keys, and—"

"Now please don't lie to me like that, sir!"

"I ain't lying. The combination don't amount to a hill of beans. The two padlocks—"

"You son of a bitch, you're just wearing me out. *Open that safe!*"

With a sigh, the banker led the way through the railing to the vault. It did take two keys, but he had both. Two enormous hasps spanned the steel door, and he knew which key unlocked which, by the feel. Raitt heard the hasps clang softly as they dropped.

"Do you need a match for the combination, sir?"

"I need a light of some kind."

"Just one match, sir. You be ready!"

No trouble with the combination, but the vault was smaller than Raitt had expected. It would not hold both of them, but at least the door was hinged to swing out to block the view from the street—if any fool was there to view it.

"I'll light one more match now. First, we want your new gold coins, if you please."

"There ain't any new gold. There ain't five hundred dollars in cash in this whole bank!"

Raitt said, "Mr. Porter, last evenin' I killed Mike Banterman and his nigra foreman. They'd drawed five hundred in new eagles and doubles from this bank. Now, you trying to tell me that cleaned you out? You got a shipment of this year's money in! You're just begging me to kill you, ain't you?"

The banker sobbed softly as he leaned into the vault and fumbled for two small canvas bags. "This is all there is. This one tens—this one twenties."

Raitt hefted them. "Do just fine, sir. You see, you didn't lie very good, did you? Now lean into that safe again one minute, please. I won't hurt you!"

The banker leaned into the safe with his back to

Raitt. It was coming on daylight fast now, and this part of the job permitted the banker to see Raitt's face. He hung the rifle in the crook of his arm while he tied the mask across his face. He had sent Eph to rob some shanty's clothesline of an old gray dress the night before.

"Now you can turn around. We'll close the door, but don't bother with them padlocks."

"What you going to do with me now?"

"Nothing to fear. You been a good man in a bad spot. Banterman and his nigra, they had to show off, but you're doing just fine! Get me a piece of rope or good stout string, sir."

Porter found a length of quarter-inch rope. Raitt told him to lie down on his back under the table. He used Porter's own handkerchief to make a gag across his mouth.

Now came the tricky part, which meant putting the rifle down. He whistled a low whistle, and Eph groped his way into the dark bank. "Stand right there, and don't speak," Raitt told him. "Can you see this banker man from there? I'm going to tie him here, like I said. If he makes any trouble while I'm doing it, you kill him."

A few minutes later, they were untying their horses in the willows. Raitt could suddenly think of a hundred reasons why it would be perfectly safe to kick open the door of a saloon and take a bottle. The look on Eph's pimpled face, in the cold, gray daylight, changed his mind. He still needed this kid.

"How much did we get, Mr. Raitt?" Eph said.

"Plenty! No time to count it now, though."

"You mean to carry it, too, like the rifle?"

Raitt put one of the sacks of gold coin inside the other, and held it out to Eph. "You're full of rabbit blood all of a sudden, boy. Why? You done well! Now what ails you?"

"You got my gun. You—"

"Yes, I have, and I mean to keep it, and I told you why. You're too green for this life, boy. They's some jobs you can do, and some you can't. You'll learn, sho'ly you will, but it takes experience. I'll tell you something else, too—we're going to get you a different horse."

"We are, like hell!"

"A plain dark horse, with speed and bottom. We'll wait until we're across the line in Mexico, and pick you up a good horse there."

"When do I get my rifle back?"

"When we're closer to Hermosillo."

"Why Hermosillo? I never heard about nothing there I keer to see."

"Gold, kid! I'll show you more gold down there in Hermosillo than you ever dreamed of. I don't know how much we got here. Couple thousand dollars, at least. Maybe more, but it ain't a caution to what we'll pick up down there."

"We got a couple of thousand dollars?" Eph cried.

"At least that much. Now didn't I tell you I'd take care of you, boy?"

Raitt wished he could remember what kind of Indian mined gold down there in Mexico. Slaves, Bru Hawley said they were. It was almost on the tip of his tongue, and it would impress this half-wit kid.

Impress Eph it would have, but the wrong way. The very word "Yaqui," which Raitt envisioned as "Yackee," would have terrified Eph into defiance. He had grown up on tales of the terrible Yaquis and would have been more afraid of them than of Raitt.

For the time being, Eph was the leader and Raitt the follower. Only Eph could get them across the Rio Grande. Riding hard, they crossed a corner of New Mexico and turned south. They splashed across the narrow river, and were in Mexico.

Raitt studied the terrain thoughtfully. Nothing that Bru Hawley had said had prepared him for this grim, barren desert.

"How come you know this trail so well, Eph?" he said.

"I worked for a man that bought cattle here."

I bet he bought them, Raitt thought. Stole them, is what he done. . . . "What happened to him?"

"Mexican firing squad shot him."

"How come they didn't shoot you, too?"

Eph's eyes dropped. "Well, I reckon because I was just a kid. I reckon that's why."

No, it was because you turned him in, that's why. You sold him out, Raitt thought. . . . "How fur is it from here to Hermosillo?"

"I don't know." Eph gave him a defiant look. "Bobby would know. He was raised down here."

"Bobby who?"

"Fayette. My pardner."

Raitt stared at him so long in silence that Eph became uncomfortable. His eyes dropped. Raitt said, "You and Bobby was heading for Mexico? Where was you going to get the money to go there?"

"Well, we was going to pick up a few horses, and take them over."

"Bar M horses? Eph, you poor fool, it's a good thing I came along! You and that sot kid couldn't steal a nanny goat and get away with it. Where could you sell horses down there?"

"Parral. Hidalgo del Parral."

"Is that near Hermosillo?"

"No, Hermosillo is in Sonora, toward the coast. Parral is in Chihuahua. I never been either place."

"Let's go."

He nodded Eph to take the trail ahead of him. If anything, the country grew drearier. Early in the afternoon, they came to a tiny, one-room shanty made of mud bricks, with a dry corral about it. Four fine horses were in the corral, but the lean, surly Mexican who came to the door appeared to live there alone.

Eph bargained with him for some food, with two dimes from Woody Brown's pocket change. They squatted under a gaunt little tree while the man prepared the food over a fire in the middle of his floor.

"Christ, is this all he's got?" Raitt said when they were served. "Red beans and corn pancakes—why, this is cabin grub! This is what you feed nigras!"

"You better get used to it. It's all you'll get down here. Look, like this."

Eph showed Raitt how to make a scoop of his *tortilla* and eat his spoon with his beans. Their host came in, watched them with twinkling eyes a moment, and said something to Eph before he went out.

"You talk Mexican pretty good, all right," Raitt said. "He kept looking at me and saying something."

"'*Gringo.*'" Eph smiled. "It's what they call an American. He wanted to know if you had a fly up your nose."

"What's that mean?"

"That's what they say when they can see you don't

like something. You listen here, Mr. Raitt, even if you
don't like things down here, you better be a little po-
liter about it. Git yourself in trouble if you want to,
but don't you get these people mad at me."

"We'll watch that; thanks." Raitt had to make himself say it. "I reckon we better rest the horses a mite
more, and catch some rest ourselves. You keep an eye
out while I catch me some sleep."

Eph got a gloating look, as though saying to himself,
At last . . . ! Raitt made himself comfortable on the
ground, with his back against the tree and the big rifle
across his lap. In a few moments, he seemed to be sleeping deeply.

Just to be sure, the kid picked up a small rock and
tossed it toward him. It hit the ground some four feet
from where Raitt lay. Raitt opened his eyes a little, and
smiled sleepily.

"Don't try it, Eph," he said.

CHAPTER NINE

The buzzards alighted boldly the minute Hawley had ridden off to town. The bodies of the dead men were well covered, but the dead horses were not. Three times, Clyde Fox drove the buzzards off when the sickening racket they made drove him crazy. The third time, he emptied his gun at them without hitting one.

Twenty seconds later, they were back. Clyde was almost weeping as he caught his horse, fitted his boot unhandily into the stirrup, and swung up into the saddle. He did not know where he was going—only that he could stand no more of this.

He reloaded his gun as he rode. He gave no thought to the money that Mike Banterman owed him—a whole summer's wages, a little more than two hundred dollars. No power on earth could have made him face Mrs. Banterman to ask for it, or even to take it from her hand.

His worst fear was that Woody had said something to Mike about the trouble they had, and that their lateness in getting back from town was somehow connected with that. Suppose that old sheriff knew about it. Before Mrs. Oaks died, last spring, the Bantermans and Oakses had been family friends.

Suppose Casey Oaks learned that Clyde had been talking freely about Mrs. Banterman. Suppose Woody told him that he had half choked him to death for it and had had to threaten him with the knife to shut him up. Or suppose Bru Hawley blabbed about what he had said just this morning.

I ain't to blame, no wise. No wise! Clyde kept telling himself. But it'll all come out now. . . .

He had worked for Mike for two years. A good job, and he was heartily sorry that he had spoiled it by his smart-aleck talk. There had never been any reason for it. Mrs. Banterman wouldn't spit on him, and he now knew it. Being Mike's pet, he had just seen too much of her. More than was good for him.

Clyde knew the country. To the west, there was nothing. South was Mexico, unknown to him, and fearful. North lay the Bar M, and he was fleeing on a Bar M horse.

His only chance lay in heading for Louisiana. Get rid of the horse as soon as it had served him and he safely could. Get a job somewhere and pile up a little money. Change his name.

Let's see; I'll be Tom Anderson. No, I knowed a Tom Anderson once. What was that man's name that

me and Tom worked with? Something Boyd. I'll be
Tom Boyd. . . .

His horse saw the man on foot before Clyde did. He
reined in without thinking. He knew the man, because
Bobby Fayette had once worked a while for the Bar M.
Most men who came through here did. Bobby had not
lasted long.

Clyde deeply needed a friend who was in as much
trouble as himself, and Bobby usually was. He was a
drinker, and obviously he had been tying on an over-
load. He was so wild-eyed with misery he was half
out of his mind. The heel of one boot was gone, and
he had puked all over his clothes.

"Hey there, Bobby! What you doing out here
afoot?" Clyde said.

"Got any water? Christ, I'm dead for water," Bobby
croaked.

"No, I ain't got any water. Let's see; where'd I go to
fetch some?"

"Take me up behind you!"

Bobby lurched toward him. Clyde spurred his horse
aside, shouting, "No you don't! I don't know as he'd
carry double."

Bobby simply buckled at the knees and fell on his
face. Clyde slid out of the saddle and knelt beside him.
Bobby's slack-mouthed pallor frightened him when he
turned him over. He was barely breathing.

For a moment, Clyde forgot his own problems, and when he thought of them again, it was to decide that finding another dead man was riskier than helping Bobby. Yet it was not pure self-interest that made him try to put Bobby on the horse behind him. In his nitwit way, Clyde Fox had kindness in him.

The horse had no intention of carrying double. Luckily, Bobby came to in time to help himself. The nearest place Clyde could think of where there would be water was Pat Patterson's place, northeast of town. His was a two-bit spread for sure, but water was something he had.

Clyde made elaborate plans for what he'd tell Pat when they got there, but luck was with them. Pat and Flavia and the kids were gone. Bobby revived after he had gulped down a little water. Clyde found a can and milked one of Pat's cows, and Bobby revived still more when he had retched down the warm milk.

"You still ain't told me how come you're afoot out there, Bobby," Clyde said.

It was not very clear in Bobby's mind, but he tried. Couple of weeks ago, he and Eph Crippen had burglarized a store in some little crossroads town over near Odessa. They got a little food and a silver dollar, and Bobby's horse was shot out from under him, getting away. They had been one-horse fugitives ever since.

"That Eph can't do nothing right," Clyde said wisely. "What happened to him?"

"Oh, he took up with somebody else and put me afoot," Bobby replied.

He did not go into details. He talked ramblingly of the plans he and Eph had had for making money by selling horses in Hidalgo del Parral, Chihuahua. As far as Bobby was concerned, Eph was out in the cold now.

"Hey, you lived down there, didn't you? You can talk their language. Is there work for a man down there?" Clyde said eagerly. It did not occur to ask where Bobby and Eph planned to get the horses to sell.

"In Chihuahua?" Bobby saw Clyde's interest, and his own chance. "Say, they're always short of men down there. Of course, you've got to know how to get across the river, and then it's a long old ride to Parral. They raise the finest horses in Mexico there. They—"

"Let's you and me go, Bobby!"

"Riding double?"

"Oh, hell, we'll take one of Pat Patterson's horses!" Clyde said recklessly. "Come on, Bobby! A poor man hasn't got a chance around here. You know one thing sure—*I* ain't going to let no pardner down and put him afoot like Eph Crippen. Come on!"

Raitt and Eph had ridden in silence for more than two hours after leaving the shanty where they had eaten. The thirst had come on Raitt suddenly, and with blinding intensity. He had never needed a drink worse than he did now, stranded in the middle of nowhere with this pimple-faced, white-trash kid.

He reined in suddenly and called out, "Eph!"

Ahead of him in the trail, Eph looked back. "What?" He reined in too.

Raitt's lips were stiff, he needed a drink so badly. His tongue worked slowly, too.

"How soon we hit the trail to Hermosillo?"

"This is it."

"Oh, hell! You're lost, kid, that's what."

"No, this is it."

"Then why are we heading south? What kind of a damn fool do you think I am? Don't know east from south!"

Eph got that stubborn-rat look. "I ain't going to no Hermosillo, God dang it, Mr. Raitt!"

"I see. Then where are you going?"

"Hidalgo del Parral."

"Why?"

Eph was frightened, and when he was frightened, he shouted. "Because I can get three hundred dollars for this horse down there, that's why! They'll pay almost anything for a good paint. You give me my rifle and my half of the money, and you go to Hermosillo if you want. But, by God, I'm going to Parral!"

"No you ain't, you little son of a bitch!"

"Go ahead and shoot!" Eph shouted, as Raitt slowly drew his gun, shifting the weight of the rifle to his left hand. "What'll you do then? You cain't even talk the language here!"

It was Raitt who saw them first, but it was Eph who recognized Bobby Fayette, riding bareback on a strange horse. He tried to shout a warning at Bobby as Raitt jumped from his horse and loosed the safety on the rifle.

Bobby saw Raitt drop to his knee. He tried to throw himself off the horse, to make a less conspicuous target. The slug caught him below the heart and knocked him backward over the horse's rump. He lived for a few seconds after hitting the ground, but he did not know it.

Raitt stood up and waved the gun overhead with both arms. "You!" he called to Clyde Fox. "Come forward with your hands up. Look smart now!"

"How can I hold this horse, with both hands up?" Clyde called back, almost weeping. "Oh, Jesus, man, don't shoot, don't shoot!"

The horse that Bobby had ridden ran only a few rods before stopping to browse on the brush. "Get off your horse and lead him," Raitt called. "On the double, there! Eph, go catch that other horse. Easy does it now, boy! You know I'll blow you in two before you can ride out of range."

Seeing Fayette knocked back that way was as good as a stiff drink to Raitt. He was back in command again, making the white trash step smartly. He stood there with the Springfield at the ready as Clyde plodded toward him and as Eph captured the Patterson horse and led it back by the reins.

"Why, I know you!" Raitt said with a wide and brilliant smile. "You's the boy with Banterman, ain't you?"

"Yes." And oh, God, Clyde thought, there's the gun that killed him and there's the man that done it. I knowed it, I knowed it . . . !

"What you doing here in Mexico?"

"Just—just—just—"

"Don't choke up like that, boy! Where you headed?"

"Parral. Someplace like that."

"No you ain't. You're going to Hermosillo. Eph, which way is the Hermosillo trail?"

"Yander, beyond the mountains, Mr. Raitt."

"What mountains?"

"Them."

Eph pointed. Raitt saw a dim purple line in the sky. His eyes dropped from it to Eph's vacant face, and then went to Clyde Fox's. Two of the scaredest faces he had ever seen.

"What's your name, boy?"

"Clyde Fox."

"Clyde Fox, *sir*."

"How's that?"

"Both of you boys better start saying 'sir.' Discipline, discipline! Three of us, and four horses. All we need— discipline and plenty of horses. All in favor of me being captain, say 'aye.' Go on, say it!"

"Aye," said Eph.

"Aye," said Clyde. He had the feeling that he had gone crazy and was only imagining this.

"You lead the way to Hermosillo, Eph," Raitt said. "Fox, you fall in behind him and lead the spare mount. One thing you both better understand right now, I don't sleep much and I don't sleep heavy. It's something you learn in war, boys. You understand that, now? Speak up!"

"Yes," said Clyde.

"Yes what?"

"Yes, sir."

"Move out, boys."

They moved out. Yes, sir, two of the scaredest white-trash boys he had ever seen in his life. Only one thing bothered Raitt as he dropped in behind them on his little hotblood mare. No one had told him that there were mountains between him and Hermosillo.

CHAPTER TEN

Senator Chidester did not leave for Austin, after hearing of the murder. His sympathies were all with Casey Oaks. There was no question about the job in the auditor's office now, with Mike Banterman dead and no longer a threat to run for Congress. More to the point, Casey did not make many close friends, and Mike had been one of them.

The banker had been almost dead when he was found. Casey had been unable to talk to him, but Francis B. Skeane, the cashier, could tell him the amount of the loss. Casey immediately left town with a posse, heading for El Paso and the border.

He was back shortly after noon, having found no sign of the fugitives. "They're long gone across the border by now," he told the senator. "I hope Eli's in shape to talk, now. See if I can get a description of this booger from him."

"I'll go with you," Chidester said.

They found the banker in a rocking chair, still in slippers, pants, and dressing gown. "Can't you wait until he feels better?" Mrs. Porter said. "His nose plugs up on him when he lays on his back. They just about strangled him, tying him there."

The banker's wife was a plain-faced, flinty-eyed little woman that Casey respected and liked. "Sure, Alma, I can wait," he said. "But for every minute I lose, these men gain an hour."

"You ain't going to catch them nohow."

"The bank will put up a reward, surely, and so will Velma Banterman. I hope the state of Texas ain't too cheap to offer its share, too. Money talks in Mexico, same as it does here."

He held up a crumpled rag, a piece of faded gray gingham. "Found this out back of the bank. Does this look like anything you ever seen, Eli?"

"That was the mask he wore," the banker said.

"Ever seen dress goods like this, Alma?"

Mrs. Porter took it and examined it. "Flavia Patterson had a dress like that. I don't know anybody else."

"That ties things together. Anybody running from the murder of Mike Banterman and Woody Brown would go that way, to dodge town. Eli, what can you tell us about the man you saw?"

Porter described him as best he could. A big mustache that bulged his mask. Eyes a queer shade of light brown, almost yellow. Gaunt of build, stood erectly like a soldier, but raggedly dressed.

"Could you tell where he hailed from by the way he talked?"

"Floriday maybe, or Georgia."

"Not the Virginia Tidewater?"

"No, I've knowed Virginians. This was a cracker from a middling-poor family. Why?"

"The man I'm thinking of took offense at being called 'Tidewater,' and I wonder why."

"It's been my experience that not everyone that claimed to be a Tidewater aristocrat planter can back it up. Now this man, he had the manners. Everything was 'please' and 'sir' with him, but I bet he's just a cracker that never ate light bread until he left home."

"Now this rifle of his."

"A brand-new Springfield .45-70."

"That's a gun I'm not familiar with, Eli."

"I am. I've seen them."

"All right, we know how our man is armed, and we know where he hails from. All we have to do is get close enough to him to make sure where he's going to die. That may take some doing."

The senator could not help but think what a peerless lawman had been lost to the Texas Rangers when Casey Oaks stooped to steal from a dead prisoner. Anyone who took that hard face and those agate eyes to represent a mere heavy-handed gunman, underrated their man.

"You seem pretty sure it's the same men that killed Banterman and Brown," he said.

"How many outlaws do you think I've got licensed to operate in my county?" Oaks said. "See here, all they got from Mike and Woody was what Mike was going to pay his crew with. Francis Skeane tells me he paid Mike in new gold coin. If you've ever been around payroll robbers, what does new gold coin mean to you? Why, a fresh shipment of gold, that's what it means!"

"I see."

"The cracker with the mustache, he's the boss. The other one was maybe somebody that worked around here. Somebody Eli would recognize—somebody that knowed the town well enough to know the path through the willers that Eli took to the bank."

"I just can't think who it would be," the banker said feebly.

"Well," Casey said angrily, "they had all the nerve they needed, to go up there and knock on your door that early in the morning."

"They didn't knock on my door. There was this pair of tomcats fighting out there in the weeds, and—"

"*What?*"

"A pair of tomcats, making an awful racket. I was afraid they was going to wake Alma, so I went out and hollered at them. And this fella, he just leaned over the porch railing and rammed this gun into my belly."

The sheriff reached for his hat. "Take good care of him, Alma. I don't know if we'll get his money back or not, but it sure won't help if Eli has a long sick spell over this, you hear?"

Senator Chidester had to hurry to keep up with the sheriff on the way back to the courthouse. "Think you know the other man now?" he said.

"Sure! Worthless little bastard is sure-enough in bad trouble now."

"Who is he?"

"Name of Ephraim Crippen. His daddy's a no-account loafer around here, but it won't do no good to talk to him. Eph run off a year or so ago. He'll be long gone to Mexico by now. He used to work for a cattle buyer who bought cows in Chihuahua. At least he claimed he bought them."

"At least you're no longer entirely in the dark."

Casey did not respond. They reached the courthouse, and the sheriff unlocked the door of his office and held it open.

"I won't stay long, Case. I reckon you're none too sure of catching these men?"

"I wouldn't bet a dime I'll catch them."

"Then I reckon you'll want to think things over before I talk to the Governor."

"Think what things over?"

"What I'm to tell him. Or even if I'm to see him on your behalf."

"Why, tell him I want Ferris Terry's job!" The sheriff balled his hand into a hard fist. He smiled with real humor, and his eyes lighted up as he added, "Or I'll be forced to run for Congress myself. You tell him that, Aubrey—I'll run for Congress myself."

"You can't bet a bluff with His Nibs."

"How is it a bluff, Aub?"

"Why—here you are, two murders and a bank robbery, and you don't expect to solve either case. A record like that won't make you much of a platform to run on, Casey."

There was a real twinkle of laughter in the sheriff's hard eyes. "It's hard lines, all right. All a county sheriff can do is grind his teeth, the law leaves him so helpless. What kind of state do we live in if all you've got to do is skip into Mexico after you kill two people and rob a bank? Do you know the circumstances under which I can cross my own county line? Only if I'm in hot pursuit of a fugitive. Hot pursuit! And I can cross into Mexico only with the consent of the appropriate authorities there."

The senator looked at him admiringly. This man was far from being a typical country lawman! "So this puts it up to the Texas Rangers, you figure?"

"I'll tell you something about politics in a small

town. If you can give people an honest answer, they'll respect you, even if it's a bad one. It's the questions you can't answer that wreck you."

"I don't quite follow you, Casey."

"The story about the man that got up in a public meeting and asked the candidate, 'Can you tell us exactly when you stopped beating your wife?' He didn't accuse the man of beating his wife, see. But how can you answer a question like that? Anything you say is wrong.

"Colonel Crawford and the Rangers can't no more catch these two men than I can, and I know it. But it's now their job, not mine. I wish them luck. You just ask the Governor this one thing, Aub. When did Colonel Crawford stop beating his wife?"

"I don't think I'll go back to Austin just yet," the senator replied.

He was there late the next morning, in the sheriff's office. Both men were writing letters, the sheriff at his own desk, the senator at the deputy's, when the door of the office was opened diffidently. A nondescript young rider stood there, waiting to be told to come in or stay out, one or the other.

"Hidy, Hawley," Casey said, looking over the tops of his spectacles. "You're early to town."

Ah yes, the senator thought—the young fellow who first brought news of the murders.

"Yes, sir. Wonder if I could talk to you a minute or two," Hawley said.

"I told you to stay there and lend Mrs. Banterman a hand."

"That's what I want to see you about, Sheriff. I talked to Mrs. Banterman last night. What she needs is a manager. I couldn't run that place! I want to talk to you about something else."

Casey put down his pen and put his spectacles in the case. "Come on in. Pull up that stool there. Now what do you want to talk about? No, no," he went on impatiently as Hawley glanced over at the senator. "This is my old friend, Senator Chidester. If I can trust him, I'm sure you can."

Hawley sat down on the stool. "No question in my mind, Eldon Raitt done them killings."

"And robbed the bank, too."

"I want to go after him."

"So you want to go after him?"

"Yes. The way I see it, onliest place he could go is Mexico. He ain't never been there and don't talk the language, but I think I know where he'll head. Hermosillo. That's where we was going when the work ran out at the Flying M. He was just purely loony about it, Sheriff. He was cold all the time, and when I told him it was warm down there, it's all he could talk about. I bet anything, he'll head there."

The sheriff leaned forward. "Well, well, and now you want to go after him!"

"Yes. Mrs. Banterman said go ahead. She said to ask you about putting up a reward. If you say it's all right, she'll put up five hundred dollars. That's enough to nail him to the highest cross in Mexico. Only one thing, Mrs. Banterman don't want him killed. She says he's got to be brought back to stand trial. She don't want no more useless killings, Sheriff."

"That sounds like her."

"Yes. She's a real nice woman, Sheriff. I—I feel like since I come there with this bastardly Raitt, the least I can do for her is bring him back."

"You think you can do it?"

"I got a better chance than anybody. I was brought up down there. My daddy run a cow ranch for some English people. I'll be among friends there."

The sheriff said, in clumsy border Spanish, "But first you've got to get there. It is many, many miles to Hermosillo, across high mountains. This man has a long rifle, remember!"

Hawley replied in Spanish so perfect that the senator had trouble following it: "He can't shoot me if he doesn't see me. Moreover, he doesn't sleep well, and he has no strength. My plan is to get ahead of him and wait for him in Hermosillo, among my friends."

The sheriff switched back to English. "You talk it like a native. You're probably right—that's where Raitt will head. The kid that's with him can speak the language—not well, not even as well as I can. But well enough."

Hawley smiled and shook his head. "That's Yaqui country. They'd just as soon skin you alive and feed you to the ants as not, and border Spanish ain't going to help. My daddy worked Yaquis. I got friends there too."

"But the *rurales*, them federal range police—you know how to get along with them, too?"

"As much as anybody can."

"The reward might help there."

"I thought of that."

"The bank will put up five hundred dollars, plus 10 per cent of all the money that's recovered. Add that to Mrs. Banterman's five hundred, and that's a heap of bandit-bait."

Hawley fetched a sharp breath. "Jesus, yes!"

The sheriff leaned back in his chair, put his hands behind his head, and looked across at the senator. "What do you think, Aubrey?"

"I think he ought to have the color of legality if he's fool enough to take such chances," Chidester replied.

"You can't commission a private bounty hunter. Your writ doesn't run that far."

The sheriff opened a desk drawer and took out a cigar box full of badges. "My posse arsenal," he muttered. "Never been useful yet, but you never can tell. Hold up your right hand, Mr. Hawley."

Hawley got up off the stool and held up his right hand. The sheriff stood up and recited the oath rapidly, from memory. Hawley repeated it after him, swearing to defend the Constitution of the United States and that of Texas without fear or favor, so help him God. The sheriff handed him a bright, new badge.

"Pin that on you, at least until you're across the line," he said. "How you fixed for money?"

"Not a cent."

"Go to the bank and tell Mr. Skeane that I said to advance you a hundred dollars in five-dollar gold pieces. Then you eat something, and better grain your horse, too. Shouldn't take you more than an hour and a half. Let's say now, you be back here at four on the dot. We might as well leave tonight."

"We?" Hawley cried.

"Why, sure. I'm going with you," said Sheriff Oaks. "You didn't think I'd let you go down there by yourself, did you?"

CHAPTER ELEVEN

The sheriff left the preparations for the trip to Hawley, who kept them simple. They stowed .45 ammunition everywhere about their persons and saddles. He bought ten pounds of raisins and four one-gallon, blanket-covered canteens. He showed the sheriff where it had been his custom to hide his own money in little slits cut in his saddle and the double tops of his boots. The sheriff cut a few in his own, and all but fifteen dollars of the bank's money was thus hidden. The sheriff carried one five-dollar gold piece and some five dollars in change. Hawley carried only five dollars' worth of American and Mexican coins in his pocket.

The departure was undramatic. Only the senator, the deputy sheriff, and some stray dogs saw them off. "I hope you know what you're doing, Casey," the senator said.

"So do I. It's a job for the Texas Rangers, but by the time they unravel the red tape it's always too late. You ask the Governor that question—Aub—when did Colonel Crawford stop beating his wife," Oaks said, and there was no twinkle in his eye.

"I can't decide how serious you are about this man hunt."

"Way I like it. Let's go, Hawley."

They rode in silence through what was left of the day and through most of the night. The sheriff rode in the lead, but he was aware at all times that Hawley was pushing the pace behind him. They made good time. At dawn they were in El Paso.

Casey pulled his horse down and let Hawley catch up. "You aim to go right on across?" he said.

"The earlier the better," said Hawley.

"Horses are getting tired."

Hawley cleared his throat deferentially. "Way I figure it, Sheriff, we better ride mostly at night. We can rest the horses somewhere on the other side."

"Why ride at night?"

"Well, I don't much fancy riding into range of that booger's rifle in broad daylight. Way I see it, we've got to get ahead of them quick, and you even things up a little in the dark."

"First we got to get across the river."

Again Hawley cleared his throat. "I wish you'd let me try my luck getting us over. They ain't going to like the idee of a *gringo* sheriff man-hunting in their territory, and there ain't no way you can pretend to be anything else. If you'll excuse me, just don't get on your dignity, or act weapon-heavy, and let me do the talking—"

"See here," the sheriff said. "I ain't quite a complete damn fool. If I didn't need somebody like you to get me across, I'd've been long gone down there. You're in charge now."

"I never quite know how to take you."

"Nothing slippery about me. You just figger how a plain, simple man would think, and you'll have me figgered out every time."

"That is the damnedest lie I ever heard."

The sheriff did not respond. They walked their horses through town. Hawley took the lead as they started across the wooden wagon bridge across the Rio Grande. In the stillness of early dawn the slow hoof-beats of the horses boomed like funeral drums.

On the south shore of the river were a few small adobe buildings and a corral. There was no sentry in sight, but a non-commissioned officer quickly mustered a squad of five men before they were halfway across the bridge. By the time they were on Mexican soil, an officer came out of one of the adobe buildings, pulling up his pants.

They were small men, dark of skin, tough-looking, wearing the odds and ends of several kinds of uniforms. Only the officer wore shoes. They were armed with everything from one brand-new .30-30 carbine to old smooth-bore muskets. The officer wore a pair of pearl-handled .45's on crossed belts.

Hawley reined in without waiting to be stopped and threw the officer a sort of sloppy salute. His jocular, low-voiced greeting was not returned. Casey could not understand half that was said, but it seemed quite clear to him that Hawley was not at all offended by the officer's attitude, which ranged from disinterest to suspicion.

Hawley was saying something like, "We have to bring back two murderers before they disgrace us by killing innocent Mexicans. It is sad, but we will have to insist that you allow us to avenge our own shame. It is a matter of honor, do you understand?"

"Do not try to teach us about honor," replied the officer. "In Mexico we have our own honor, and our own way of dealing with two foreign murderers."

"In Mexico it is not good to interfere with the honor of another, as I know."

"What! You teach me about Mexican honor? What do you know about Mexico?"

"Enough. It was my milk-mother. I may look like a *gringo*, and talk like one, but—"

"No, you talk like a Mexican. That is one thing I don't like, when you pretend to be a Mexican."

"I did not pretend to be a Mexican. I said only that my honor is a Mexican thing. You can kill me, but you cannot kill my Mexican honor, which makes me hunt these two murderers until my last breath. Then there is the money."

"What money?"

And so on. Hawley slouched sidewise in the saddle, his voice soft and sleepy-sounding as he explained that the American law as well as his own sense of honor would not permit him to touch blood money. Part of the money might have to go to the Yaquis, part to the *rurales*. He was honor-bound to pay them for their help.

But there would be plenty for the soldiers who so bravely guarded the border, too. When Hawley got out his cigarette papers and tobacco, and the officer held out his hand for them, the sheriff was fairly sure the argument was won.

Hawley came to the time when it was politic to introduce the sheriff. Oaks knew enough to lean out of the saddle, offer his hand, and say, "*Con mucho gusto, Señor Coronel.*"

The officer smiled and said, in perfect English, "Only a captain, Sheriff. You pass on, and have good luck. Try not to get killed."

Again Hawley saluted sloppily. No one returned it. They rode on. Their horses had rested a little as they walked, and were ready to canter again. In a few hours they saw a little one-room shanty creeping toward them. As they came closer, they made out a small corral with several fine horses in it. A man came out and watched them approach.

"You just play ignorant, and let me talk this time," Hawley said. "Calling that captain a colonel was all right, but it don't work everywhere."

The sheriff listened, and again only half understood what he heard. One thing he did understand—Hawley had learned the trick of speaking in such a low voice that the other man had to strain a little to make it out. It gave the other fellow something extra to think about, and put him at a disadvantage.

They breakfasted on *tortillas* and beans, and paid the man with a few bunches of raisins. "Line camp," Hawley explained, as they ate. "His job is to turn back strays and watch that nobody don't steal cows. It's a punishment job, for fighting. He's going crazy with lonesomeness."

"I feel sorry for him," Casey said, "but has he seen Raitt and Crippen?"

"They et here yesterday morning."

"Which way did they go?"

"South, toward Hidalgo del Parral."

"Hell!"

Hawley smiled. "But he spotted them again this morning, yander. They changed their minds and turned east."

"That's a relief."

"He even seen that long gun Raitt carries. And that fool Crippen is riding a flashy paint horse. They're just asking somebody to steal that gun and that horse."

"That's something we've got to think about. Somebody beating us to them."

"Here's something else to worry about, too. This morning, there was another man with them, and they was leading a horse. Do you know a brand that's kind of like this?"

Hawley sketched it in the dirt with his finger. "Looks like a Broken W, Pat Patterson's brand," Casey said.

"Mean anything to you?"

"Possibly. If you're coming south from the Bar M and circling east to miss town, you'll cross Pat Patterson's range. That seems to be where they got the dress goods to make Raitt's holdup mask. How about the other horse?"

"It was a Bar M."

"That goddam worthless, mouthy Clyde Fox, maybe."

"That's the way I figger it. I reckon we better catch us some sleep, Sheriff."

"Safe to sleep here?"

"One at a time, anyway. I'd just as soon do it that way from now on. You want to sleep first?"

"No, you go ahead. You get to my age, you want a little time to get awake in the morning, and a little more time to get ready to sleep at night."

Hawley stretched out on the ground, pounded his hat into a sort of pillow, rolled over on his stomach with his face on the hat, and went instantly to sleep. This kid is all right, the sheriff decided. Well, I'm entitled to some luck. . . .

CHAPTER TWELVE

The high purple line in the sky crept closer day by day. It came and went, came and went, and at times had depths and dimensions of mountains. They had been climbing slowly for three days. Now suddenly the skyline of mountains disappeared, and the tilt of the land became steeper.

Raitt had never been in better shape. His only concern now was getting through the mountains. There always seemed to be a choice of trails. That decision was Eph's, and Eph had turned out to be not a bad man at the job. They were on a well-traveled trail now. It went somewhere.

Eph rode in the lead, on the pinto. Behind him came Clyde, leading the extra horse. Raitt brought up the rear, with the .45-70 balanced across his little mare's withers.

Eph dismounted, almost without slowing down the pinto. He walked for a considerable distance, leading his horse. The dejected Fox neither noticed nor cared. Eph turned suddenly and held up his hand.

"Better rest them horses," he said. "It's coming on a mighty sheer climb. I'd unsaddle, too."

"He ain't even blowing," Clyde complained.

"He will be. Wipe his back down, before it gets sore. Neither one of you takes good enough care of a horse for this country."

Eph pointed to the broken country that rose ahead of them. The purple and gaudy gold had vanished. It was all dun-colored canyons studded with hot gray rocks. Beside the trail, only cactus grew.

Raitt dreaded dismounting. He knew that sometime he would get out of the saddle and not be able to get back into it. But he swung one stiff leg over and dropped to the ground, letting the butt of the rifle hit the ground first.

"That's right, Eph. Man's got to take care of his mount," he said. "Stand down, Clyde, and wipe your horse down."

"Nothing to wipe him down with," Clyde said, dismounting.

"You've got hands, haven't you? Hell of a trooper you'd make! No barn men to do your work out here. Let's see the gristle in you, now. Get that saddle off, and look smart!"

Clyde stripped his horse and began pushing the sweat off its back with the flat of his hand. Eph cared for the pinto, and then, at a curt nod from Raitt, came back to take care of his mare.

"What do you call this horse, Mr. Raitt?"

"Call her?"

"Yes. Ain't she got a name?"

"Her name is Lottie. Why?"

"I never heard you say it. A horse don't mean very much to you, does it?"

"I never rode a poor horse in my life. What's the matter with you, boy?"

Eph's look was almost insolent. He was tough-looking and gaunt. Even his pimples were gone. "Nothing's the matter with me, only it ain't right to use a good horse and not really care about it."

"What do you want me to do—kiss her?" Raitt pulled the mare's head up sharply, and kissed her on the cheek. "That make you happy?"

Eph did not reply. He stripped the mare's back of sweat, let her cool out a little, and then put the saddle back on her.

"How fur to the top now?" Raitt said.

"I don't know. I told you, I ain't never been this way before."

"Can't be far, though."

"Looks a right smart piece to me. What worries me, we're following two horses that's shod all around."

"What about it?"

"Few Mexican horses is shod on all four feet. They're lucky if they're shod in front."

"It worry you?"

Eph nodded. "I keep thinking, what if it's Sheriff Oaks?"

Raitt hung the rifle under his arm. "He's out of his jurisdiction here. This is what has got the jurisdiction here," he said, patting the rifle.

He tried to fit his boot in the stirrup, and discovered just how tired he was. He knew Eph was watching closely for a chance to grab the rifle. He turned deliberately and looked him in the eye.

"There now, give me a hand up, boy, and don't just stand there with your mouth open, catching flies! I ain't as young as you are."

Eph cupped his hands together. Raitt put a foot in them and swung up in the saddle. He smiled down at Eph.

"Thank you. I don't like to pick at you, Eph, but by dad, if you can't be aggravating sometimes! What did I tell you about taking care of each other?"

"I could lighten your load of that rifle."

"You could try," Raitt said softly.

They rode on. Sometimes Raitt dozed in the saddle, resting with his eyes not quite closed. The slightest change in the pattern of shadows registered on them, bringing him awake. He might doze off again immediately, but both boys knew by now that, separately or together, they were not going to ambush him as he slept and overpower him.

Their one chance was to kill him, and this they lacked the ferocity to do. They needed him. They needed his adult shouldering of responsibility. They needed his decisiveness. They needed to have their minds made up, not just once in a while but several times a day. They were more afraid of the unknown future than they were of him.

Also, he had the money. He had never discussed the money since Clyde Fox joined them, and he was pretty sure that Eph and Clyde had never talked about it. But Eph knew that Raitt had it, and Clyde at least knew about the money taken from Banterman and Woody Brown. While he had the money and the rifle, he held their futures in his hand.

Eph pushed the pace a little harder. Several times, he got off to walk and search the trail. Clyde rode dejectedly, his mind a thousand miles away. The trail grew steeper.

In the afternoon, occasional scrubby little pine-like trees appeared. High above them, Raitt now and then could make out the darker green of larger trees behind the haze that hid the mountains. Then suddenly they were surrounded by the stumps of small trees in every canyon.

Thousands of stumps, tens of thousands of stumps! And here Raitt felt a little tug of wind, neither cool nor damp, but certainly not the searing breeze they were used to. It came from the west, and Raitt's thirsty body felt the sea in it.

Raitt stood up in the stirrups. "Hey, kid, what kind of trees are these? How come they're cut?"

Eph was hiking along, leading his horse. He stopped and looked back. "*Piñones*. I hear they was cut to make charcoal to work the mines."

"Then we must be getting close to Hermosillo."

"Why?"

"Why, that's gold country."

"I never heard of no gold there. That's cow country."

Oh, this white-trash whelp has got a lesson coming . . . ! "You just get us there. I'll find the gold for you."

"You come here, Mr. Raitt. I want to show you something."

Raitt spurred his mare ahead, making Clyde move out of the trail. He did not dismount. "What's the problem now?"

"Look at these tracks."

"The two shod horses? We knowed they was ahead of us, didn't we?"

"But look at the old tracks underneath. Mules and burros."

"A pack train?"

"I was thinking more of Indians. What if it's 'Paches, Mr. Raitt?"

The name of that tribe that Bru Hawley had mentioned came back to Raitt. "Oh, pshaw, what would Apaches be doing here? More likely Yaquis."

"They're just as bad. Worse, maybe."

Raitt felt a sharp tug of uneasiness, but it would not do to let Eph suspect it. "Oh, bother! You make a heap of trouble over nothing, boy."

"You don't know nothing about Yaquis, Mr. Raitt. Let me tote that rifle now. I'm the one has to go ahead."

"No, and you know why. I can't take a chance you'll lose your head and shoot your best friend."

Eph got that pouting look of boar-pig obstinacy. "It's my gun, God dang it. You promised me!"

"No, Eph. I think you might take a notion to kill me. Now I *know* I'm not going to kill you, and I know you're the best tracker I ever seen. So we'll go on just like we been doing."

"No, you ride point, then!" Eph shouted, losing his head. "I ain't going into no Yaqui country without my Springfield—not one goddam step!"

Raitt said, coldly but patiently, "Any Indian laying in ambush, I'll see him from back there before you will.

You'll get your rifle in Hermosillo, and this is the last time we're going to talk about it, understand?"

He won, as he had known he would. Riffraff like Eph had not the pride to withstand pride. Eph mounted and rode on.

The hours passed. The pinto played out suddenly on a short, sharp grade. It dropped its head and spread its legs, and Eph tumbled from the saddle with a sob.

"Look at him! Look at my horse," he bayed brokenly, fumbling at the saddle cinches. "He's done fur. Onliest good horse I ever owned, and he's dead!"

Raitt's mare had cocked her ears forward and was snuffling the air. "Take it easy, Eph," Raitt said soothingly. "There's water not fur ahead. Look at my mare!"

"She smells something, sure enough," Clyde said.

"Yes. Give Eph a hand, and I'll try to scout out some water. Boys, we're almost there! See what happens when we take care of each other?"

He did not know what he was going to do when he rode on up the trail, leaving the two disheartened boys behind. If they were really close to the top, he had no further need of them. That gave him a choice—get out of range of a .45, where it was two against one, and drop them with the rifle. Or simply abandon them and ride on.

He found a small but steadily flowing spring shaded

by twisted, scrubby trees of some kind, five steep miles up the slope.

He also found something that changed his mind about disposing of the boys. It was a bloody rag, the sleeve of somebody's shirt, used to make a bandage and then thrown away after a wound was washed. The blood was not quite dry.

He drank and watered his horse. He filled his hat with water and started back down the trail, leading the mare. Soon he met Eph and Clyde. Eph rode the extra horse and led his pinto. Clyde followed on the Bar M horse in his usual slack-faced daze.

"I'll tell you the truth, Mr. Raitt—I sure never expected to see you again," Eph said in a gush of emotion after all had drunk at the spring.

"You thought I'd leave a trail pard?" Raitt said reproachfully. He touched the bloody rag with his boot toe. "What do you make of this?"

Eph and Clyde did not lose heart as much as he had feared. Filling their bellies with water had restored their nerve, and the sly sea breeze came more often now and was stronger. They stretched the rag out and examined it, and it told them nothing. A shirt of checked blue gingham, neither brand-new nor old. Neither remembered having seen such a shirt before.

Eph walked back down the trail alone, and came back at dark without having learned anything. "Then don't fret yourself," Raitt said. "If anything to worry us happened down there, you'd see it."

"No I wouldn't. I ain't that good a tracker. All I can tell you is, them two shod horses went past here and are still ahead of us."

They decided to spend the night at the spring. There was no feed for the horses, but it could not be helped. They ate the last of the supplies that Eph had bargained for at a little ranch the day before. Cold *tortillas* that had gone stiff and dry, and were like munching shingles, and only three each.

The two boys went to sleep. Eph moaned in his sleep like a little boy, but Clyde slept like the dead. Raitt slept sitting up with his back against the bank beside the spring, the rifle across his lap.

It was Raitt who heard the tinkle of a bell, from the west, coming down the slope. He stirred Eph awake. The kid sprang up like a scared wolf. Raitt shook his arm.

"Sh-h! You hear that? A pack train, I'd say. Stir Clyde out and get the horses out of sight, and then you come back here to palaver with whoever it is. I'll cover you with the rifle."

The boys dragged the horses out of sight. Clyde remained with them. Eph returned, and walked up the trail until Raitt called to him to stop, just before he went out of sight. There was no moon, but the stars lighted the trail amazingly well.

The bell came closer and closer, and then a single mule came into sight, followed by a man afoot. The mule bore a high, teetering pack. It seemed to know where it was, since it began to shuffle faster as it neared the spring.

Eph called out something in Spanish. There was a little exchange of alarmed discourse between him and the mule driver, and then Raitt saw them draw close enough together to shake hands.

"Come on out, Mr. Raitt," Eph called. "He's just a peddler, is all, and by God, he's got some candy he can sell us!"

The Mexican was a young man, burly of build and muscular, but apparently glad to find himself among friends. His eyes bulged at sight of the Springfield when Raitt came out carrying it at the ready in his right hand.

Eph did the bargaining. For a half dollar from Woody Brown's pocket, they bought four pints of rice for their horses and about a pound of hard candy. Nothing Raitt had ever eaten tasted better.

"Ask him if he's got any whiskey or rum, Eph," he said.

"Now Mr. Raitt, you don't want anything to

drink," Eph said, getting that stubborn, boar-pig look again. "Wait till we get to Hermosillo."

"Goddam you, ask him if he's got any whiskey or rum!"

"That's the first thing he tried to sell me. All he's got is *tequila del norte*."

"What's that? I've drunk tequila."

"It's aged tequila that comes down from Jalisco. It's supposed to be the best, but Mr. Raitt—"

"How much does he want for it?"

"He wants five American dollars for a little old bottle, but—"

"Tell him we'll take it. Here, you boys take the rest of my candy."

The Mexican handed over the bottle, accepted the gold piece, watered his mule, and hurried off down the slope in the dark. Clyde went back to get their horses, which he tied again near the spring. The boys munched candy greedily as they fed the horses the rice, from their hats.

The bottle held a little more than a quart, so far as Raitt could judge. It was so tightly corked that he had to dig the cork out with his knife. He sat down with his back against the bank again, the rifle across his lap, and took a drink.

That first wonderful drink! Raitt made it a small one, to make it last.

Eph and Clyde finished with the horses and curled up to sleep in their old places. Raitt did not feel the need of sleep. Every now and then he got a bad shivering fit as the sea breeze became stronger and colder, but the tequila warmed him nicely.

He knew exactly when Eph would make his move, somehow. When the fire of a thirst was on him, Raitt's brain was sharpened by alcohol. He became all brain for a while.

There was no way for Eph to get behind him. Eph furtively slipped off his boots while he pretended to sleep. He rolled over, lay listening a moment, and rolled over once more. Again he listened, as he pulled his feet up under him.

Eph jumped. Raitt drove the cork back into the bottle, dropped it, and threw himself on his back on the rifle. For an instant, Eph's face was no more than a foot from Raitt's. He got his grip on the barrel of the rifle and pulled.

Raitt tilted his .45 up and squeezed the trigger. The muzzle blast showed him Eph's face as it became nothing. The slug caught him in the nose and did more damage to him than the rifle slug had done to Woody Brown's head. He did not so much as quiver after he fell.

Clyde Fox came awake screaming. Raitt pulled back

the hammer of the gun again, but Clyde never got off his hands and knees. Raitt let the hammer down, holstered the gun, and reached for the bottle. "I don't get that drunk," he said.

CHAPTER THIRTEEN

Sheriff Oaks had gathered enough twigs and leaves for a tiny fire, which he ignited when he saw Hawley coming up the slope toward the spring. Over the fire he had hung a stick holding the last five strips of the dried beef they had bought, somewhere far back on the trail.

"Too bad we ain't got some coffee," he said as Hawley dismounted. "You look like you could use some."

"I sure could." Hawley led his horse to the spring and let him drink.

"Any sign of them?"

"They're a fur piece back. I reco'nized that paint horse, though. Remember that place where the trail lays right in the bottom of the canyon?"

"Yes."

"It'd be a cinch to waylay them there, if you just wanted to gun them down. I don't see no way to take them alive. They have the aces on you, with that rifle."

He tied the horse by its halter rope and came to the fire. The sheriff said, "They're going back to hang in Texas. Better eat something. You look done in."

Bru looked at the leathery strips of beef that were twisting and shriveling over the fire. "Ain't much left, is there?" he said.

"You eat it. You been doing most of the work. I'm too tired to be hungry. A few more days of this, and I'll be done in too."

"You was the one wanted to come along."

Casey did not reply. Bru slid a strip of meat off the stick and munched it slowly. Already the little fire was going out.

"Finish it up," the sheriff said.

"I had enough."

"I said, finish it up!"

Bru took the stick, pulled another piece of meat from it, and threw the stick at the sheriff. "You eat it. Who the hell do you think you're talking to?"

"I'll split it with you." The sheriff broke the stick in two, and handed Bru the end that still had two strips of meat. "Where'd you learn to track?"

"I didn't," Hawley said in a surly voice. "We had Yaquis on the ranch. They did the tracking."

"Ever been on a man hunt before?"

"Twice."

"Who was you hunting?"

"The first one was an American that worked for my daddy. He beat a Mexican to death with a club. The other one, a Mexican rider stole somebody's daughter. Yaquis ran them both down."

"What happened to them?"

"The first one, Daddy had him hung. Daddy made the other'n marry the girl." Bru grinned. "He was afraid of getting hung, too. It sure wasn't no act of mercy when he wasn't."

"I take it you never been married."

"I never been bit by a mad dog, either."

The sheriff sat down and leaned back on his elbow. "I talked the same way at your age. I didn't get married until I was almost thirty. I'm glad I waited. I appreciated it more, and I had more to appreciate. She only lived fifteen years. I wouldn't take fifteen million dollars for them years."

"Nothing lasts," Hawley said. "There ain't nothing on earth that's worth the trouble."

"That's a penny-ante way of looking at things."

Hawley stared at him sullenly. "Seems to me we're out on the same dry trail, sleeping on rocks with an empty belly. What did it get you? Tell me that, Sheriff. What did it get you?"

"Well, if you're too damn—"

"*Sh-h!*"

Hawley shot to his feet and stood listening. It was late in the afternoon. Soon the sun would go behind the mountains, and the sharp evening chill would come down. The sheriff, hearing nothing, thought regretfully of the long night's sleep he had planned to enjoy here. From now on, Hawley thought, it would no longer be necessary to travel at night.

"Keep the horses quiet," Hawley said. "I'll go have a look-see."

The sheriff pulled the horses together, and ran his arms through their halters so he could clamp his hands down on their noses if necessary. He heard it clearly then—the tinkle of a bell, far up the slope to the west. Pack horse, he thought. Somebody trying to make the spring before nightfall. . . .

Hawley went almost out of sight before dropping to his knees behind the first rock big enough to hide him. The tinkling bell became louder and louder. Hawley could squat there with the patience of an Indian, not moving a muscle.

First a jaded little white horse came into sight, two people riding bareback. Behind them came the mule that wore the bell, bearing a high, teetering pack. The mule driver followed on foot.

Hawley let them come to within twenty feet before standing up with his gun in his hand. He let them hear him double-cock the hammer, before calling out in Spanish:

"Stop! Stop there, and tell me who you are. We are friends. Who are you?"

The sheriff left the horses and hurried up the trail to join Hawley. One of the persons on the old white horse seemed to be a woman. She sat sidewise on its withers, enveloped from head to bare feet in an old dun-colored *serape*.

The man behind her was a mountain of fat. He was dressed in shabby black, with bright ornaments on his hat and the wide belt that cut into his thick body. Tin or silver—tin, probably, the sheriff decided, noticing the man's gray hair. Some elderly village sport who still fancied himself a ladies' man.

The fat man spoke sharply to the mule driver. The mule driver plodded his mule past the white horse. He took off his hat and smiled ingratiatingly.

"We are friends too. I am a trader, called Enrique Delgado. These persons are Jesús María González, called Molacho, and his wife, Trinidad."

"Where you going?" Hawley said.

Delgado shrugged. Again he smiled. "I go everywhere."

Hawley looked at the fat man. "You—where do you go?"

"To visit my uncle. Would you rob us? Like all honest people, we are poor. We have nothing."

"That the lady will remove her *serape*, to see her face," Hawley said stolidly.

The fat man jerked the shawl from the woman's head. "Behold, a woman. What did you expect?"

She was only a girl, probably fifteen or sixteen, and her tawny face was the saddest the sheriff had ever seen. She was barefoot. Her slim body was clad in a shabby dress too long for her. It had once been white. It was a caricature of a wedding dress, a rag.

He remembered that "molacho" meant "toothless." The fat man's smile showed many gold teeth, but no goodwill. The sheriff said, "Watch it, Hawley. This may be another one of them girl-stealers."

Hawley merely nodded. He jiggled his gun at the mule driver. "Walk on down the trail, that I may talk to your friend, the toothless one."

Casey saw, almost too late, that the mule would pass between the fat man and Hawley. He started to scramble up the side of the canyon, to where he could cover Hawley.

Over the top of the mule's pack, he saw the fat man slide a mean-looking little hand gun out of his shirt front and press it against the girl's head. "Don't move!" he said. "I swear before the Mother of God, I will kill her if you do. Now—take off your guns, the two of you. Drop them!"

"Don't do it," Hawley said, in English. "He can't watch the both of us at once. He—"

He got no further. The girl moved like a panther.

She slid off the white horse, shot under its belly on her hands and knees, and was gone.

Casey was starting to unbuckle his gun belt. He went for the gun instead.

The fat man fired twice, before the mule got out of the way and the sheriff could shoot. He saw the flesh jump where his two slugs pounded into the fat man's chest. The fat man made no sound as he pitched to the ground.

Casey got to Hawley's side just as the youngster's knees buckled. "I'm all right," he said.

"Lean on me," Casey said. "It's no disgrace to hurt a little. Go ahead and groan!"

Hawley did not lose consciousness. The girl helped the sheriff stretch him out on the ground, to examine him. The wound that had frightened the sheriff—the one in the chest—was trivial after all.

The fat man's gun had seen better days. It was no more than a .32, and the little slug had barely penetrated between two ribs. The sheriff was able to get it between his knife point and his thumb, and pluck it out almost bloodlessly.

"More breech blast than muzzle blast, lucky for you," he said. "The one in your hind end is going to hurt, though. That's all good red meat."

"Ask that peddler if he's got anything to drink. Give

me a shot of something," Hawley said, the sweat suddenly drenching his face, "and cut her out!"

"That's the way to take it, yes it is. You remind me of myself at the same age."

"Get me something to drink. My goddam leg is going numb!"

How heroic these kids felt, with their first wounds! But if you survived, nothing was ever again the same. It was a touch of death, which never again looked like such a slut.

The girl was clutching Hawley's hand, urging him in rippling Spanish to be brave, trust in God, and receive her thanks for saving her life. Hawley's eyes rolled wildly, and he cursed the sheriff for his slowness in a low-pitched snarl.

The sheriff made the peddler open his pack. He had only a quart of tequila, but it was smoother-smelling stuff than the sheriff was used to. He gave Hawley a drink from the neck of the bottle.

"Now be patient. I'll have to hone up my knife for this. This one's deep," the sheriff said. "Turn over, and let's get your pants down."

"Get this goddam girl away from here!"

"Pshaw, let go of them pants. This is going to hurt, and it ain't going to make a scar you can be proud of."

The bullet had struck high in Hawley's hip just as he pivoted. It had entered at the side, but the sheriff thought it could more easily be reached from behind. He and Hawley quarreled sociably as he whetted his knife on his boot.

"Now look at the fix we're in!" said Hawley. "You ain't going to take them men alive now."

"Why ain't I?"

"Why, you old fool, I'll be laid up for a week!"

"Longer than that, but I ain't helpless."

"Oh, hell, you potbellied old fool—you against three of them, with that Springfield? All you can do now is waylay them. If you take the gun and the horses back to Texas, that's proof enough."

Casey put his knife down, picked up the bottle, and started to pull the cork to give Hawley another drink. "Say! Didn't you tell me Raitt is a drinker?"

"Yes, but—"

"How fur do you think we can trust this peddler? If we could get him to sell this liquor to Raitt, it'd do us more good than if you drank it. How hard a drinker is he, really now?"

Hawley forgot his wound a moment. "I only seen him get drunk once, and they gave us knockout drops before he really got going. But he wanted it so bad, Sheriff, he was shaking like a leaf. You felt sorry for the poor bastard, the way he was shaking."

The sheriff pointed the knife at him. "All right, you tell this peddler to go on down there and act like nothing happened. Tell him to sell this tequila to them for anything he can get. If he lets on he's seen us, he's as good as dead—make sure he understands that."

"No, let them come here, to the spring, first," Hawley said. "We'll take the peddler with us and turn him loose farther up. Let them bed down here for the night."

"I reckon that is better."

"First, cut this goddam bullet out, before I lose a leg!"

"All right. But this is going to hurt."

The girl made a little weeping sound, as she saw the small hole where the bullet had gone in, and the darker, rapidly swelling bruise where, the sheriff thought, the bullet now lay.

"Let me. I don't think you know how to do it. My mother taught me," she said imperiously.

On a hunch, he handed her the knife. She drove it into the flesh of Hawley's rump, making him go rigid from head to toe with the effort of not crying out. The sheriff could hear the point of the knife grate against something.

She pulled the knife out, drove it in again. Hawley buried his face in his arms and said, "Ah-h-h!" The sheriff noticed what a vivid red Hawley's blood was, on the small, tawny fingers of the girl.

She brought the bullet up triumphantly on the point

of the knife, and held it out to the sheriff. They poured cold water from the spring into the wound the girl had made, and she pressed her hand against the wound until she forced water out of the tiny entrance hole.

They rolled the body of the fat man down the canyon, out of sight. By the time they were ready to start back up the trail, Hawley had regained command of himself enough to give instructions to the peddler. His voice was hoarse, and he ran out of breath easily.

But he made an impression. "If you betray yourself, they will kill you. If you escape from them, we will follow you and kill you. What you must do is simple. Sell them the tequila, and then leave! Is that not better than being killed?"

The mule driver vowed he would be wise, as well as loyal and brave. They kept him until almost dark, and then watched him go off down the trail behind his mule.

"Only way he could double-cross us is to slip around the spring and not even stop there," the sheriff said.

"Ah, shut up," said Hawley.

"In the daylight, maybe he could do it. I don't see how he can in the dark."

"What good is it going to do to get him drunk? You can't take the three of them alive! All you'll do is get yourself shot."

The reaction had set in, and the deep, fiery pain. A wound at this stage was humiliating rather than heroic. Ah, it was hell to be young! Casey watched the girl lean over Hawley and wipe the creases in his forehead with her fingertips. She made a little cooing sound, deep in her throat.

"I said I'd take them back to Texas," Casey said, "and I'll have to give it a try. Did that fat man with the gold teeth steal this girl?"

"How the hell do I know?"

"Ask her."

Hawley's question loosed a torrent of words in the girl. Hawley averted his face. "She said yes, he did," he growled. "A man three times her age. He bought her this wedding gown, and when she wouldn't have him, he waited until she was alone in the house and stole her."

"Seems like quite a bit of that goes on here."

"Why do you plague me? Let me sleep!"

"Sure, you go to sleep, Hawley. Seems to me I've heard that if you save a Mexican's life, he's under obligation to you till the end of his days. How does that work out when you save a girl's life?"

Hawley did not answer. Poor devil, the sheriff thought, he's got her on his hands now, and he's just Mexican enough himself to take it seriously. You can't get away from the way you was raised. . . .

Not long after darkness fell, he heard a single gun-shot from down there beside the spring. It did not sound to him like the big Springfield. More like just a .45.

That one shot, and then silence. It was going to be a long night. "Tell her to keep her ears open and wake me up if she hears anything," the sheriff said. He lay down and went to sleep. The last sound he heard was the girl's voice telling Hawley that he would soon be well and strong again.

CHAPTER FOURTEEN

Clyde Fox lay curled up on his side, his face toward the dim silhouette that Raitt made. He had heard the deadly, soft clicking and clacking as the madman reloaded that one empty chamber in his gun, after killing Eph. Now and then he heard a light grating sound that he identified as the big rifle rubbing over Raitt's belt buckle every time he moved.

That was how he thought of Raitt—a madman. From Eph, he had had snatches of confused description of the deaths of Mike Banterman and Woody Brown. There had never been any mystery to Clyde about those deaths, but hearing it from someone who was there overwhelmed him with awe and horror.

All night the cool sea breeze blew from the west. Clyde tried not to shiver, because every sound of movement disturbed Raitt. Despite his terror, he kept drifting off to sleep and then waking himself up, sobbing and moaning. The next sound was always Raitt, stirring around there beyond Eph's body, never speaking, prying silently through the dark to see what Clyde was up to.

Toward daylight, Clyde drifted off into the deep sleep of exhaustion. While he slept, the wind reversed itself, rising from the desert to the east to pour through the mountain passes in the offshore gale the Mexicans called a *chubasco*. Clyde had turned on his back as he slept. He awakened drenched with sweat.

The first thing he saw was the buzzards that spiraled over their heads. He remembered everything instantly, but still hoped it had been a nightmare. He looked over and saw Eph's body, he remembered the buzzards that had circled over the bodies of Mike and Woody, and the horror came back.

"You crying?" came Raitt's voice.

Clyde turned his head and saw Raitt, who had surely not been long awake himself. He had stood up to relieve himself, but he carried the Springfield under his right arm as he buttoned his pants. His face was puffed and swollen, especially around his eyes, but he was far from being drunk.

"You answer me. You crying?" Raitt said. "Set up there and talk, boy!"

Clyde sat up. "I guess I was having a dream."

"You ort to be fixing us something to eat."

"There ain't nothing to fix, Mr. Raitt."

A slow, stiff smile spread across Raitt's face. "Only too true, only too true!" he said. "Now what you looking up for, manna from Heaven?"

"Them buzzards, Mr. Raitt. We better bury Eph, don't you think?"

"Why?"

"Them birds will give us away, if anybody's follering us."

"Is that a fact!"

Raitt was not being sarcastic. He actually did not know about buzzards. He looked up briefly. "All right, you cover him up. We're going to rest here a while, beside this here spring. It can't be fur to the pass now. We'll start up in a little while, and make it over the summit before nightfall. Then it's downhill all the way to Hermosillo."

"You—you figger to take me to Hermosillo too?"

Raitt did not bother to answer. Clyde found a relatively soft place below the trail, closer to the bottom of the canyon, and scraped out a shallow grave with his hands. When he went for Eph's body, he saw that Raitt had already taken Eph's .45. It was a sickening job, the worst ordeal of Clyde's life, to drag the body down the slope and then cover it with dirt and rocks.

He returned to the spring. The buzzards kept wheeling overhead, and now one or two came slanting down into the canyon. At first they soared swiftly back up again, riding the stiff desert wind. But he counted and saw first one, and then three more, that vanished and did not come back again.

"Mr. Raitt, look yander!" he said.

Raitt had sat down beside his bottle, which seemed to be still a third full. He removed the cork, wiped the mouth of the bottle ceremoniously with the hairy back of his hand, and took a slow, stilted drink of several small swallows.

"Look at what?" he said, replacing the cork.

"Them buzzards. There must be something else dead down there."

"I ain't lost no one near and dear. Have you?" Raitt said with his ugly smile.

"Well, but, Jesus, even if it's nothing but a jack-rabbit, they're going to call attention to us."

"You're correct about that," Raitt said, with a sage nod. "Tell you what. You go bury whatever it is."

"Why don't we just ride on?"

"Why don't you do as you're told? You and me have been getting along just fine. Now what do you want to go and spoil things for? Go see what's dead down there, and look smart!"

Clyde did not descend to the bottom of the canyon. He came toiling back swiftly, out of breath, with teeth that wanted to chatter.

"It's a dead man, a big fat man in black pants and shirt, Mr. Raitt."

"Who is he?"

"How the hell do I know? Some Mexican."

"You didn't bury him so fast, did you?"

"Jesus, no. I don't want to bury no more bodies. Goddlemighty, Mr. Raitt, let's get out of here!"

"Now boy! We found a bloody rag here last night. We slept here all night, and nothing happened, did it? Now you found where it come from. I declare, you's the timidest boy! I tell you truly, a dead man can't be half as much trouble to you as I can."

Clyde thought, Go ahead and kill me, you murdering, cold-blooded son of a bitch, and get it over with. . . . He stood there and watched as Raitt picked up the bottle and took one more small sip, drinking slowly, as a gentleman should. When Raitt put the bottle down again, Clyde's heart broke. He turned and ran, at considerable risk of a broken leg or back, all the way to the bottom of the canyon.

The black-clad dead man was already drawing ants by the million. They were in his half-open eyes, his nostrils, his mouth. The strange thing was that the buzzards had not yet attacked. Five big, black ones— the biggest Clyde had ever seen—paced back and forth a couple of rods away, waiting.

Waiting for what? This canyon was dry as a buffalo bone now, but in the flash floods that sometimes broke over the desert, it carried water enough to move boulders that weighed several tons. It dawned on Clyde that the body had not *fallen* against one of these big boulders. It had been *dragged* there after death.

I ain't going to spook now, and get myself killed for that son of a bitch of a Raitt, Clyde told himself, fighting down sheer panic. Go galloping around that rock, and that's just what'll happen. But I do aim to see—I *got* to see—who's on the other side, that them buzzards can see and I can't. . . .

He picked his toe hold, hooked his boot into it, and held his breath as he mounted the top of the rock. He went down on his belly and inched forward, and suddenly found himself staring into the gun and the hard, tired, lined, and sunburned face of Sheriff Casey Oaks.

CHAPTER FIFTEEN

She's got her rope on a *gringo*, Casey thought, watching the girl's watchful, brooding care of Bru Hawley—now let's see her throw and hogtie him. . . . It could have been entertaining to listen to all night, except that it brought back too many painful memories. It did not seem possible to the sheriff that he had ever been that young himself.

Yet he had indeed been, as his own cruelly treacherous memory proved. Days of hot, hard work that he thrived on, nights when he either risked death, running after some girl as young as this, or his sanity by thinking of her. A good thing the young were so strong, the reckless way they squandered their strength.

"Goddam it, let me alone!" he heard Bru snarl in English with a throat dry and constricted by pain.

"*Si, Señor. ¿Quiere una bebita de agua?*"

"No, I don't want no goddam drink of water!"

"*Si, Señor. ¡Cálmate, cálmate!*"

Bru refused to speak to her in Spanish, and she accepted it meekly, as one did the lunacies of men, and went on smothering him with kindness. Calm yourself, calm yourself! As though a man with a wound in his hind end could be anything but half mad, at twenty-whatever it was that Bru was.

The sheriff felt no need of sleep. All he wanted was to get this ugly job done and get home, where his enemies would miss him if his friends did not. Instinct told him that, every day he was away, the danger to the entire edifice of his life increased.

But that's a chance I took, and I knowed it when I took it. And if I lose, I lose. It sure is the truth; not even penitence squares you for some mistakes. You pay and pay and pay. . . .

Toward daylight, he got up and stretched himself and tried to summon up the old wake-up vigor with which he had greeted so many, many dawns. It refused to answer his summons. He would start this day flat-footed, instead of on tiptoe. Getting to be more and more of that, these days.

The girl was squatting beside Bru, with a corner of the *serape* around her shoulders. The rest of it covered Bru. "*¿Duérmele?*" the sheriff asked her, softly.

"*Si, Señor,*" she said, but Bru snarled, "No, I ain't asleep. How the hell could a man sleep with both of you stomping around all night?"

Casey went over and stood looking down at him, wishing for a fleeting split second that he could be young enough to feel that kind of pain again. No, it wasn't worth it. . . .

"Your rump pretty sore?" he said.

"It ain't my rump; it's my leg."

"Then why ain't you sleeping on your back?"

Bru almost howled, "I was shot in the side of the leg. I got cut in the hind end because you two blundering fools didn't know no better. If you go back there and tell it around that I was wounded in the hind end, so help me God I'll fix you!"

"I wouldn't do that. If I's you, Hawley, I'd tell people that an *alacrán* bit you there. Yes, sir, you set down on a scorpion, that's how you got decorated in the behind."

"You think you're so goddam funny. I could just die laughing at you, Sheriff. You ort to go on the stage, you're so funny."

"It ain't so funny when you think how far we got to go to get home. Even if I can take this cuter in today, how long before you'll be able to ride?"

"*¡Cálmate, cálmate!*" Trinidad said as Bru began writhing.

"You try to take him alive," Bru said, "and you'll just get killed. Then where the hell am I? Use your God-danged head, Sheriff! Get a bead on that son of a bitch and don't take hard chances with him—gun him in the back if you can!"

"We'll see, we'll see," Casey said soothingly. "I'm going to see what I can see there now. If he ain't drunk, we may have to think of something else."

No use saddling his horse. He groped his way down the trail afoot, thankful it was downhill. He missed his breakfast. He missed, as a matter of fact, all the meals he had not eaten since leaving home.

It was farther than he had thought. He stopped every now and then to listen, and heard nothing. It was broad daylight before he came in sight of the spring. The last cover was too far from the spring for him to see anything clearly. He had to leave the trail and pick his way, a methodical step at a time, up the wall of the canyon.

He had not noticed the buzzards himself until he found a comfortable lookout above the spring. He could see Raitt sitting there with the rifle across his lap and the bottle beside him. The disheartening thing was the slow way Raitt was drinking.

No man could drink that much tequila and not feel the effects, but it seemed to him that Raitt was one of those drinkers who could pace a bottle. He would finish it, but he'd stay on his feet, too.

Every word they said came to the sheriff clearly.

"Them buzzards, Mr. Raitt. We better bury Eph, don't you think?"

"Why?"

"Them birds will give us away if anybody's foller-ing us."

"Is that a fact! All right, you cover him up. We're going to rest here a while, beside this here spring."

Poor Eph, the sheriff thought—he drawed nothing but deuces his in-tire life. . . . Thing to do was get down there and take Clyde Fox first. He began work-ing his way back the way he had come, and although it was downhill now, it was slow, hard going.

By the time he had crossed the trail and had circled the spring without showing himself, Clyde had made a grave of sorts for Eph Crippen. But the buzzards had found the body of Molacho and would not leave. Casey was too far from the spring to hear the discussion be-tween Raitt and Clyde this time.

But he saw Clyde pick his way down to the bottom of the canyon, looking back over his shoulder and grumbling shrilly under his breath. Casey got there first. He could tell by the sound of Clyde's breathing when it dawned on Clyde that a living human being was all that could keep the buzzards from a dead one.

He was ready when Clyde tried to slip up on him by coming over the rock rather than around it. He rammed him in the face with the muzzle of his gun, catching him just under the eye and tearing a hole in his skin.

"Shut your mouth! One sound out of you and I'll blow your head off," he hissed.

Something came over Clyde's face, aging it, making it manlier somehow. He blinked back the tears that pain brought to his eyes.

"Let me down there, out of sight," he whispered. "Come on, Sheriff, make room."

The sheriff stood aside and helped Clyde down. He handed him his handkerchief to mop away the blood. Clyde was shaking all over. His eyes glittered, but not like a madman's.

"Sheriff, that fella is crazy as a bedbug. Killing somebody don't mean no more to him than for you or me to step on an ant!"

"I reckon. Can he shoot that rifle?"

Clyde's eyes rolled wildly. "Hey, dear God, he could drive a nail with it from here. Listen, I can stand him off for a while. Sooner or later, he's going to get behind me where he can pick me off with that Springfield. But if you go back down the canyon and come up behind him, he ain't going to have no idee you're anywheres near."

"And drop him from behind, you mean. No, he's going back to Texas to stand trial."

Clyde mopped at his face, smearing blood all over it. "You'll never take him alive. You don't know him! Sheriff—"

"He don't know me either, if he thinks he can get

away with a double ambush murder in my county. How much of the bank gold has he got left?"

"All of it, fur as I know. He—"

"How did Eph get killed?"

"He—he just cut him down like a mad dog."

"Last night? I heard the shot, I reckon."

Clyde started to say something, but he closed his eyes and remained silent as they both heard Raitt calling him, from up there at the spring.

"Clyde! Hey, boy, what's become of you?"

The sheriff holstered his gun and grabbed Clyde's shirt front in both hands. "Answer him! Stand him off —keep talking to him—keep him talking to you. Make him come down here after you. Don't move from here, whatever you do. I've got to be damn good and sure where you are, every second."

"I wouldn't double-cross you," Clyde moaned.

"Talk back to him!" The sheriff shook him hard, with both hands. "Make him mad. Sass him, like you think you're holed up where you could stand off the Seventh New York. And God help you if you let on anybody's with you!"

The sheriff transferred his hands from the shirt to Clyde's throat, briefly. Clyde said, "I didn't break no laws. I'm a free man. I don't have to take no—"

The sheriff slapped him across the face with his left hand. "Where is Pat Patterson's horse? I wonder if you think I'm half-witted, or what? You horse-stealing little son of a bitch, you wouldn't be the first horse thief I've hung!"

"Clyde," Raitt said, "if I have to come after you, make sure you'll sorrow for it."

Clyde shivered and rubbed the bruised places on his throat. He dropped to his knees, cupped his hands around his throat, and shouted back.

"Oh, go to hell, why don't you? You ain't scaring me a bit!"

"That's the way!" the sheriff said, in a hoarse whisper. "Keep him upset, make him sore, don't give him time to think!"

He crouched low and scuttled away. He had gone no more than ten feet when Raitt shot. Both of them cringed involuntarily as they heard the big slug from the Springfield go squalling across the canyon, high above them. Casey looked back at Clyde.

"Christ! Sounds like an old buffalo gun, a Sharps. Holler at him! Sass him back good."

"Go ahead, waste your fire," Clyde shouted. "You and me got a lot of things to settle now, Mr. Raitt, and I ain't no Eph Crippen. You wish you'd not got so gay with me now, I bet, don't you?"

Casey could hear them talking as he fumbled his way toward some kind of cover in Raitt's rear. Twice more, he heard the blast of the .45-70, and his blood ran cold despite all the things he could remember from a life-time as a peace officer when he saw that Raitt was firing into the body of the dead Mexican, Molacho.

From where he squatted then, Casey could not see Raitt until he stood up to fire, but he could see the body, with its covering of ravenous ants of all sizes. Big ants and little ones, red ones and black ones, all feasting as fast as they could while it lasted. The buzzards started to take clumsy flight at each shot, but then settled down heavily to wait until all this foolish excitement was over and they could pre-empt the body.

It would have been relatively easy to drop Raitt, both times he stood up to shoot. It was far from being point-blank range, but the sheriff knew he could have got Raitt somewhere in the body with a .45 slug. And maybe, he thought, it wasn't so bright to pass it up. These things are all right when you're younger, but—

Raitt seemed to have decided exactly where Clyde was hiding. He was not about to give up the advantage the rifle gave him, by going down there to close quarters. He stood up a moment, sizing things up with a quick, cool eye.

He turned then and started back up the slope toward the spring. Casey watched him a moment. Raitt showed the effects of the drinking, but he was a long way from being drunk. It was as though he had to do everything twice to get it done. Put his foot down wrong, and then do it right. Reach for the wrong brush to help himself, and then the right one.

Just half drunk, which was worse than not drunk at all. Some men thrived on it, were sharper with half a skinful than they were stone sober.

I'm making a hell of a lot of noise, the sheriff decided. Then it came to him: But he's making more. No reason for him to tiptoe. He can't hear me for his own noise. . . .

He hurried more boldly, not sure of where he was going or what he would do when he got there, except that he wanted to get close to Raitt somewhere up there by the spring. He lumbered along with the gun in his hand until he saw a short, heavy club. It was a pitch-laden knob from a *piñón* tree, sun-dried for years, and worn smooth in the flash floods that had carried it down from somewhere up near the summit.

He holstered his gun and picked up the club. It felt good in his hand, but while he stooped to dig it out of the sand, he lost Raitt for a moment. He dropped to his knees and wiped the sweat out of his eyes with his sleeve.

There he was, up there by the spring, calmly and a little fastidiously taking another drink. Pull the cork. Wipe off the mouth of the bottle with the back of his hand. Fingers spread gracefully over the bottle, thumb on the other side bent just so. Back with the head, and then the dainty gurgle of those frugal little sips. Bearded lips pursed, the Adam's apple dancing.

Oh, if I could only get behind him now—!

The sheriff broke from cover, shouting wordlessly at the top of his voice as he saw Bru Hawley come out behind Raitt and jump for him. Raitt dropped the bottle and swiveled on his heels to bring up the Springfield. He shot once at Bru, from the hip, but the gun had too much recoil for him. It almost jumped out of his hands, the slug going wild.

Raitt heard the sheriff bellowing then. He could not shoot both ways at once, and he could see that the white-faced, reeling Hawley was a sick man. Raitt went to his knee and hefted the Springfield to his shoulder. Hawley threw himself at Raitt and got his arms around the man's neck.

Raitt shrugged him off and aimed the gun again. Casey was still thirty feet away, running uphill, when he wound up and let go with the *piñón* club.

He had had his bad luck for the day. He caught Raitt in the face—it looked to him like plumb on the bridge of his nose—with the whirling club. At the same time, Hawley dropped on Raitt again from behind, and got his hands on the rifle barrel.

They fought for the gun for a second or two, until the sheriff got there and dropped on Raitt with both knees. "Get the hell out of the way!" he shouted at Hawley. He knocked Hawley aside with the heel of his hand, and then he got both hands on Raitt's throat and his knees in Raitt's stomach, and bore down.

"Shoot somebody now, why don't you?" he panted through his teeth. "You're a hell of a man, from a couple of hundred yards away. Let's see how you like it this close. Come on, you Tidewater son of a bitch, show me how you can fight!"

Hawley pulled him off. Hawley lifted Raitt's .45 and took possession of the Springfield .45-70. He handed both guns to the girl, who came flying out of concealment the moment Raitt was downed. I like that youngster, Casey thought. She had sense enough to stay out of the way until it was over. . . .

"I thought you was suffering so bad with your wounds," Casey said.

"I was," said Bru, "but you damned old fool, somebody's got to look after you."

"You never seen the day you could do that," the sheriff said malevolently.

Clyde Fox came puffing and panting up the slope. The sheriff was just locking around Raitt's wrist the chain he had carried all these days. The prisoner was conscious, but he was so limp he seemed to be in a trance. His eyes were full of sadness that moved the sheriff not at all. He had seen the same grief in the eyes of a dying wolf. For all he knew, maybe even a tarantula yielded up its life with sharp regret, though only another tarantula could understand.

"I helped you, didn't I?" Clyde said.

"Yes, you did," the sheriff agreed.

"Well then, if I go back with you, and take Pat Patterson's horse back, I wouldn't be in no trouble for taking him, will I?" said Clyde.

"I don't need you to take Pat's horse back. Get going!" the sheriff said, and began kicking Clyde on up the trail toward the summit afoot.

CHAPTER SIXTEEN

Senator Chidester was summoned to the Governor's office one afternoon to find Colonel Crawford sulking there. At the Governor's request, Crawford showed the senator the exchange of telegrams that had taken place between himself and Lieutenant Ahlquist, commanding at El Paso.

From Ahlquist to Crawford:

REQUEST INSTRUCTIONS AS FOLLOWS COLON SHERIFF OAKS DEPUTY SHERIFF HAWLEY ESCORT SIX MEXICAN RURALES REFUSE TURN OVER PRISONER ELDON RAITT TO MY DETACHMENT STOP PREFER DELIVER PERSONALLY

From Crawford to Ahlquist:

PLEASE CLARIFY WHY RURALES QUESTION MARK

From Ahlquist to Crawford:

OAKS STATES RAITT IS RURALES PRISONER STOP RURALES ALSO HAVE CUSTODY FOUR THOUSAND EIGHT HUNDRED STOLEN BANK FUNDS FOUR HUNDRED FIFTY STOLEN IN BANTERMAN CASE STOP MEXICAN STATUTE PROHIBITS RELEASING PRISONER OR MONEY WITHOUT PAYMENT AP-

PROPRIATE REWARD ACCORDING OAKS STOP WILL DE-
LIVER COD TO OAKS JAIL

From Crawford to Ahlquist:

DO NOT KNOW ANY SUCH MEXICAN STATUTE STOP DO YOU
FEEL OAKS COLLUDING WITH RURALES QUESTION MARK

From Ahlquist to Crawford:

RESPECTFULLY SUBMIT NO OPINION STOP RURALES HAVE
CUSTODY PRISONER SOUTH OF BRIDGE

"There's no such Mexican law!" Crawford fumed.
"There's over fourteen hundred dollars in rewards
now outstanding. Oaks is plainly colluding with those
rurales. If they're entitled to the reward, let them file
for it and wait until they're paid. We don't need a
posse of Mexican policemen riding that far into Texas
to deliver a prisoner."

"Who is this Ahlquist?" the senator said. "Seems I've
heard his name."

"He's the kid who brought in the Nesbitt gang.
He's only twenty. I'm against commissioning kids, but
the Governor overruled me. This is a case in point.
They lack judgment in an emergency."

"What do you think, Aubrey?" the Governor said.

The senator smiled wryly. "I can barely keep up
with our own case law, and I certainly can't pose as an
expert on the Mexican law. Taken as a gambling prop-

osition, however, I'd give even money that, if you push them, they can come up with a statute to cover the case."

"It's that damned Casey Oaks!" Crawford said. "He thinks he's got me with my tail in a crack."

"He *knows* he's got you with your tail in a crack," the senator said. "Giles, one of the hardest lessons in politics is how to take your licking. Why make it tough on the Governor? Why not give in gracefully?"

"The honor of the Rangers is at stake!"

"It sure is. The *rurales* have a fugitive the Rangers didn't apprehend. Never mind how they got him— never mind what they want with him—seems to me the question is whether you form an honor escort to deliver the prisoner, jointly with the *rurales*, or sit there stalemated at the international bridge."

The Governor cleared his throat. "Tell you what, Giles. Why don't you send Lieutenant Ahlquist a wire —oh, say something like, 'Delighted collaborate gallant Mexican colleagues. Escort with all honors,' and so forth."

"Governor, they have no right to come armed into the state of Texas!"

"Sure enough, but I'm not going to get into no cutting match with Casey Oaks and them *rurales* both. Next time you cross the Rio to bring back a fugitive, you might have to shoot your way out. Listen, Aubrey

—you catch a train down there and rub Case down with a little sweet butter. He's more trouble to me guilty than he ever could be innocent. Arguing with him is like shoveling fleas."

The first person the senator saw when he detrained the next morning was Velma Banterman. She stood out enchantingly in her widow's weeds, in the biggest crowd that had ever assembled in the little county seat. The people had come here to watch the prisoner brought back by their own sheriff, in stately solemnity that emphasized and illuminated the kind of justice he dispensed. Ol' Case, they said, always put on a show.

Meanwhile they had trooped down to see the Flyer make its brief stop. The senator saw Velma from the top step of the coach. He pushed through the crowd to her, snatching off his hat with a courtly bow.

"Mrs. Banterman, how nice to see you looking so well!" he exclaimed, pressing her hand.

She smiled weakly. "I wish I felt well, 'deed I do. I feel I'm at my wits' end. I've always been able to handle things before, as well as any man, I've told myself. But this is too much."

She had aged visibly, he thought. This woman would never really look old, but she now had shadows under her eyes that would never leave, and deep lines of character around her mouth that had not been there before.

"What's the trouble, my dear?"

"Mike and Woody were so—so *strong*. Both gone at once, no guiding hand left, no one to lean on, for the men as well as myself. So demoralized, such chaos, so much to learn and no time to learn it—"

She was close to tears. He took both of her hands now, and said, "What you need is a good manager. Let's put it up to Casey Oaks, shall we? I'd trust his judgment in men above all others."

"Oh, do you think he would find someone for me?" she cried. "I hate to bother him, but Mike trusted him so, and I don't know where else to turn."

He took her elbow. "You come to the hotel with me and have a bowl of hot soup and a cup of coffee. Everything looks more cheerful after you've eaten. Has there been any word from Casey?"

"They say he'll get in this morning."

"Hasn't anyone made sure?"

"Someone was going to ride out and meet them." She smiled again, not quite so wanly. "But you know how Casey is. Everybody wanted somebody else to do it. He'll get here when he's good and ready, and we can just wait!"

They leaned into the cold wind and hurried to the hotel. She talked incessantly and swiftly, like a woman who had not had a listener for a long time. Not even Mike Banterman had talked her language, the senator thought. A good man, but a child in so many ways!

They were eating at a table by the hotel door when the crowd began its pell-mell flight down the street to meet the celebrities. Merely by standing up at their table, they could see over the heads of the crowd as the cavalcade plodded silently down the middle of the street.

It was a sight that might never again be seen, in Texas or anywhere else. Yet, to the senator, the most moving thing of all was Velma Banterman's pink, girlish face and bright, excited eyes. Aha! he thought; and having come to that conclusion, he could only add, Aha!

In the lead rode Lieutenant Ahlquist, of the Texas Rangers, with three troopers. If any was as old as twenty-four, Senator Chidester was no judge of men. The cream of the crop, he thought proudly. The elite of Texas, of all young American manhood.

Such a man Casey Oaks had been when young. But Casey had been flawed. For love of his wife, he lost his honor. He violated the code, that she might ride the steam cars.

Behind the Rangers came Casey himself, looking neither to left nor right, inviting no plaudits and receiving none. Here I am, but what else did you-all expect? his attitude seemed to say.

Behind the sheriff came young Brutus Hawley, sitting sidewise in the saddle, favoring one hip. With him rode a Mexican girl, on Pat Patterson's horse. All the senator could make out of her was big, solemn eyes under the edge of an old drab *serape* that covered her head.

Next came the prisoner, on his little hot-blood mare. His wrists were chained to the saddle horn. A led horse —the Bar M horse that Clyde Fox had ridden—was tied to the mare's tail, cavalry style. The prisoner looked straight down at his hands. For him, every view led to the gallows.

Last came the *rurales*, seven of them. There could be no plain-clothes policemen anywhere in the world, in plainer clothes than these. But through their odds and ends of ragged uniforms, their worn and outmoded hats and guns and horse gear, shone a steel-hard competence. No wonder Lieutenant Ahlquist had respectfully submitted no opinion.

The last Mexican officer led a handsome pinto horse, on a long rope. Lashed to its empty saddle was a Springfield .45-70 rifle.

The procession went out of sight. The senator gave a boy a dime to carry a note to the sheriff: *When you get caught up, Mrs. B. and I would like to talk to you in the hotel.*

Sheriff Oaks strode in no more than fifteen minutes later. He went straight to Velma Banterman and took her hand deferentially, holding his hat in the other. He had lost some weight and looked tired and gaunt, but tougher, too. It became him.

"How you been doing, Velma?" he said gruffly.

"Not at all well, I'm afraid."

"What's the trouble?"

The senator cut in suavely, "Now what do you think is the trouble? She's been bearing a burden that kept two strong men busy. Whom do you know that can run a place as big as that one? Go somewhere and talk to her about it! Then, as soon as you can spare the time, I want to talk to you. But first things first. All I have for you is a message from the Governor."

Casey blinked at him. "All right, run that riffraff out of my office and wait for me there."

The senator waited two hours and a half, with the fire roaring in the stove. The first hour, the young deputy spent clearing out his desk and muttering to himself. When he went out, he slammed the door. The senator was alone thereafter.

The sheriff burst through the door with something like his old-style hustle. "Nothing like getting out on the trail to put you in shape again," he said. "I still got some belly left, but I'm going to keep it. At my age, once is enough."

"You look well hardened in, yes you do."

The sheriff sat down in his chair with a sigh. "Yes I am, Aub. It was a hell of a ride."

"Where's the other fugitive?"

"Raitt murdered him. But I brung back the one that counted, and all the money."

"Plus a squad of *rurales*."

Casey's eyes twinkled. "They didn't much care for that in Austin, did they?"

"Not particularly."

"He was their prisoner until we crossed that river. You make the best deal you can, and anybody that's embarrassed by it is just too damn clumsy for his job. The Governor made Colonel Crawford do it, didn't he?"

"Yes. You made your point. I've got some other news that didn't belong on the telegraph wires. Ferris Terry is retiring, first of the year. You can have his job."

"I be damned!"

"Yes. After all these years, vindication."

Casey shook his head slowly. "Tell the Governor I said thanks, but find somebody else."

"*What!*"

The sheriff said dreamily, "I've got other obligations, Aub. I can think of several men I could send out there to run the Bar M for Velma, but not one that could do the job she's entitled to. I was a good friend to Mike Banterman. I owe it to him and I owe it to her, to go out there and keep that place going."

"I see. At a good salary, surely."

"Three times what I'll ever make here, but I can make that place pay better than Mike did."

And, you transparent old fox, finally marry the woman who owns it, the senator thought. . . . It made him feel better about the whole world when now and then things lumbered along to a happy ending. He knew how deeply the sheriff had loved Blanche, and Blanche had appreciated the rare man she had. So would Velma. The hardest man I ever knew, the senator thought; yet, in his relations with women, so guilelessly gentle and decent and courtly . . . !

"We'll have to talk this over, Case."

"What's to talk over? I mean to do it."

"We'll have to have the right man to take your place as sheriff."

"I'll find one."

"His Nibs will want to have something to say about who he is."

"You tell him he'll still be doing business with me. What I want for this sheriff's job is just a plain, honest lawman. I had to fire this kid deputy I had. He didn't even take out the ashes while I was gone. I'll find somebody and break him in, and we'll run him. But I'll go on driving the wagon and holding the whip."

"Surely you'll take us into your confidence when you decide on whom to confer your blessing?"

The sheriff let the irony pass over his head, to glance at his watch. "Where's Hawley?" he grumbled. "I like a man to be on time."

"Time for what?"

"Me and Velma are going to stand up with him and this little Mexican girl when they get married. He wants to do it the *gringo* way. Why don't you come along too?"

"He was the one who rode in with Raitt, wasn't he? Seems to me you're going to a lot of trouble for him, Case."

"I'd've been in a hell of a shape down there without him. He's a good, steady boy. Got a lot of old-fashioned idees from being raised in Mexico. He saved this girl's life, and she helped cut the lead out of him, and they believe in them things down there. You know, fate."

"I see. And it won't hurt him a bit with the voters, to have a Mexican wife, will it? Is he your candidate, Case?"

"He's one of them," Casey said, not quite meeting the senator's eyes.

"Name one more! We're going to get Hawley, whether we like it or not, aren't we? Have you—?"

"Here they are now," the sheriff said. "You be nice to this girl now, Aub."

He got up to open the door. The girl had dropped the *serape* to her shoulders, so that it no longer covered her face. A saint, the senator decided instantly. One of those rare women who are born as adults, but who are still girlish as old women. He sprang to his feet and bowed deeply.

Hawley looked hardly different than he had that evening when he came pounding into town to report a murder. He carried the Springfield .45-70, which he leaned in the corner made by the wall and the sheriff's desk. His handshake was perfunctory.

"You talk to Mrs. Banterman about that, Casey?" he said.

"Well, no, no I didn't," Casey replied. "I'm going out there to run that place for her, Hawley. Me and the senator has decided that you're the man we want in this sheriff's job. Start out as deputy, and—"

"I reckon not. I thought you was going to speak to Mrs. Banterman! You brought it up yourself, damn it! A house of our own, a garden patch, why, damn it all—"

"Things change, though," Casey said vaguely. "I didn't plan on quitting my job, either. This is a good job, Hawley, and you'll make a good peace officer."

"No. I only went down there because—well, you know why. I ain't a man hunter. All I want is to make a steady living. If your word ain't good, I wish to hell I'd never come back with you!"

The sheriff was his old, sure self. He turned and

snatched up the Springfield .45-70. He tossed it, butt down, across the room. Hawley had to catch it or be struck by it.

"There! That gun murdered two good citizens. Nothing wrong with the gun. Good gun! All it takes is the right man behind it. Somebody has to do these jobs, Hawley. Now you take that rifle and put it to good work, and you make this a safe county to live in, and you make this county proud of you and your wife, you hear? You're already swore in as a deputy. Couple of weeks now, you'll be the sheriff. All I got to say to you is, you take that gun and live up to the best that's in you, same as I've always tried to do."

"Oh, hell!" Hawley said disgustedly. He looked down at the heavy gun in his hand, and looked up again with a sigh. "Well, all right."